"Virginia Smith's *Just As I Am* co[...]
a cast of delightfully quirky souther[...]

Author of severa[...]
Friday Afternoon Club Mystery series

"Virginia Smith's character, Mayla Strong, is as compelling as she is quirky. From her purple hair down to her leopard print unmentionables, her sense of humor and compassion for others tugged at my heartstrings and pulled me out of my conservative, evangelical comfort zone. What I found out in journeying with Mayla is that God sees past our outer adornments right into our hearts. More importantly, I was reminded and convinced that God loves me . . . just as I am."

—Jenn Doucette
Author of *The Velveteen Mommy:*
Laughter and Tears from the Toy Box Years

"Purple-haired, nose-ring-wearing Mayla Strong is a character I will never forget, and Virginia Smith's *Just As I Am* is a keeper of a novel! Though by turns hilarious, heart-tugging, and convicting, Mayla and her friends illustrate the important spiritual truth we often forget—that God loves each of us just as we are and that Christianity isn't about rules but about relationship, both with Jesus and with our world. I highly recommend it!"

—Colleen Coble
Best-selling author of *Alaska Twilight,*
the Aloha Reef series, and the Rock Harbor series

"Virginia Smith brings a fresh new voice to Christian publishing in her novel *Just As I Am*. This story takes the reader into a world where not many Christians go. Showing the conversion of a young woman from that world, this book helps the reader understand the drastic changes—emotionally and spiritually—that must take place in every life when confronted by Jesus. Along the way, strong spiritual truths touch each heart. I highly recommend this book."

—Lena Nelson Dooley
Award-winning author of *His Brother's Castoff*,
Double Deception, and *Gerda's Lawman*

"*Just As I Am* is the fictional version of *Blue Like Jazz*. Virginia Smith's honest and amusing portrayal of a young woman's journey with Christ gave me a deeper, more compassionate understanding of the struggles of Gen-X and millennial Christians."

—Sharon Dunn
Award-winning author of the
Ruby Taylor Mystery series

Just As I Am

a Novel

Virginia Smith

Kregel
Publications

For my husband, Ted,
whose unwavering support
enables me to achieve
more than I could ever
accomplish on my own.

Just As I Am: A Novel

© 2006 by Virginia Smith

Published by Kregel Publications, a division of Kregel, Inc., P.O. Box 2607, Grand Rapids, MI 49501.

Library of Congress Cataloging-in-Publication Data

Smith, Virginia.
Just as I am : a novel / by Virginia Smith.
    p. cm.
1. New church members—Fiction. 2. Young women—Fiction. I. Title.
PS3619.M5956J87 2006
813'.6–dc22   2005036169

ISBN 0-8254-3693-1

Printed in the United States of America

06 07 08 09 10 / 5 4 3 2 1

Acknowledgments

My sincere thanks . . .

Every author knows that no book is written in isolation. There are many indispensable people whose names do not appear on the cover, but whose contributions are vital just the same. I am thankful to have a group of talented and supportive people who helped me tell Mayla's story.

The first is my mother, Amy Barkman, who read the first chapter and pestered me for the next two years to "finish that story!" She also gave excellent suggestions and served as a role model for the best qualities of Mayla's mother, with none of her faults.

God has blessed me with the most awesome sisters in the world. Beth Marlowe's wholehearted love of this story encouraged me more than she can possibly understand. And Susie Smith has been incredibly supportive of me and my writing from the very beginning. She even arranged my first speaking engagements as an author.

I'm grateful to my daughter, Christy Leake, for canvassing everyone she knew who had facial piercings to make sure I got the terminology correct. (Yes, even though the dictionary says a *labret* is a piece of jewelry, that's not how the term is used by those who have firsthand experience with such things.) Thanks, sweetie, for keeping me straight! Thanks also to Tambra Rasmussen, for her excellent proofreading.

Also invaluable was the excellent advice of my writer friends who slogged through the manuscript in various stages of completion: Jill Elizabeth Nelson, Julie Scott, and Michelle Shockley. And Stuart Stockton's wit and talent proved invaluable in writing the summaries, even though he would much rather read science fiction. Thanks, guys!

The entire staff at Kregel Publications has been truly amazing. I have offered more than one prayer of thanksgiving for Steve, Amy, Janyre, Dennis, Nick, Moriah, Leslie, and the many others who've been so supportive in getting this book into your hands. I am grateful to have been able to work with such a professional and encouraging team on my first book.

I am thankful for you, my reader. I have prayed for you. You have been held up to the Lord as Mayla's story unfolded and afterward, as I went through the publication process. I have asked God to bless you as you read this book, and I believe He will.

And finally, without my Lord and Savior, Jesus Christ, I have no stories worth telling. I'm honored that He chose me to tell this one.

Chapter 1

I've always said the Lord had to drag me kicking and scream-
ing to His altar, but once I got there I pitched a tent,
unrolled my sleeping bag, and made myself at home. Anyone less patient than the Almighty would have zipped up that
sleeping bag, sewn the top shut, and tossed me into the Dumpster in the back parking lot.

I'm here to tell you: not all of God's children are as patient
as He is.

I'm grateful to the Lord for a lot of things, and right up
there near the top of the list is Pastor Paul Rawlings of the
Salliesburg Independent Christian Church. When I made
my way down the aisle to the beat of "Just As I Am Without
One Plea," Brother Damon nearly choked on his gum when

he caught sight of the rhinestone in my left nostril. I swear his eyes popped out of their sockets a good half-inch when he saw the stud midway between my chin and my lower lip. But Pastor Paul never even blinked, and the great big grin on his face didn't fade. He stuck his hands out, and before I knew it, he had both my arms in a bone-crushing grip. He grinned so wide, double dimples creased his cheeks, and I got a detailed view of his back molars. I was almost afraid he was going to hug me. Being hugged by young, good-looking men is great, but not in front of a whole roomful of staring church people. I leaned back, alarmed, but couldn't shake his grip without jerking away, and I didn't think it would look right to twist out of the preacher's clutch at the front of the church.

But he didn't hug me. Just stood there grinning and squeezing my arms so hard I swore I'd be able to lift his fingerprints from the bruises by suppertime.

Pastor Paul could have welcomed me into the kingdom with a nod and a friendly handshake, but that wasn't his way. And it's a good thing, too. If he had displayed even a hint of the disapproval I could feel radiating from Brother Damon, I would have been gone in a heartbeat. I would have turned on my heel and marched straight back down that aisle.

After he finished crushing the bones in my arms, he turned me around and made me face the congregation. He had his hands on my shoulders, grinning ear to ear like he was presenting the homecoming queen to the senior class. Shock registered on every face turned my way. Salliesburg Independent Christian Church didn't see people with purple hair on a regular basis, even if they were just a half-hour's drive from the big city of Lexington, Kentucky.

"This," said Pastor Paul, "is Mayla Strong. She's Angela Strong's daughter, the one we've been praying for."

I saw a few nods, a few expressions that looked like, "Ah, *that* explains it!" and even a few sympathetic glances thrown toward my mama. Seated in the middle of the second pew, she wore the floral print dress that I always said made her look like a couch cushion. At that moment, a robin could've built a nest in her gaping mouth without having to duck to get in.

Pastor Paul turned me back to face him. "Mayla, I'm glad you've finally decided to give your life to the Lord. I know you've thought about this for a long time, and we're all rejoicing along with the angels in heaven."

Actually, I hadn't thought about it for a long time. In fact, I felt a little dazed to find myself up there in front of all those church people, ready to say the words my mama had been trying to get me to say for five years. I really hadn't planned to do this. I thought I'd follow Mama to church, sit in the back and catch a quick nap, then go up and say something to her afterward to prove that I really had been there. Mostly it was to get her off my back.

But Pastor Paul's voice wasn't easy to sleep through. He liked to use it to its fullest potential, and that man had lungs like speaker cabinets. A few of his words had seeped into my brain and started it thinking. Then they'd all started to sing that song, "Just As I Am," and before I knew it my feet were moving and they were taking me with them.

"Yes, sir," I said, not wanting to go into the whole thing right then.

Pastor Paul beamed again. "Well, we're going to take care of your eternal soul right now, Mayla. And we have the baptismal all ready, too. When the Lord moves, here at Salliesburg Independent Christian Church we like to be prepared to move with Him. Do you want to go ahead and do the baptism now, or wait for another day?"

I felt the weight of all those eyes. Wait for another day? Since I had come this far, I might as well go all the way. "Uh, let's do it. Sounds good."

The preacher's smile widened farther than I would have thought possible. "That's fine. Angela, you want to come up here and help Mayla get ready?"

Mama didn't need prodding. Before he stopped talking, she was side stepping over the ladies in her pew. In the aisle, she gave a single tug at the skirt of her dress and then jogged— I swear she jogged—up to the front where I stood beside the preacher. I was wondering what he meant by "get ready" when she grabbed me by the arm and pulled me toward a door behind the piano.

"Where are we going, Mama?"

"To get you into a baptism robe," she whispered, pulling me through the door. Once on the other side, she turned and gave me a breath-stopping hug.

"I'm so proud of you, baby!"

I followed her up a little staircase to a room behind the choir loft. In the corner stood a coatrack with several white robes hanging on it. Mama pulled one off a hanger and held it up to me.

"This will do." She looked at my blouse, deep creases between her eyebrows. "A shame you don't have something else to wear. Those tiger stripes will show through soon as it's wet."

"Wet?" A little stab of alarm knifed me in the stomach. "How's it going to get wet?"

The creases got even deeper as Mama gave me an odd look. "It's going to get wet when you go under the water."

"Go under?" My voice squeaked, and she shushed me.

"I've explained it to you before," she whispered. "It's a symbol of your fresh new life in Christ Jesus. You'll make the Confession of Faith, and then Pastor Paul will dunk you under. You go in the water as a vile and disgusting sinner, and you come out a clean and pure child of God."

It was coming back to me. She *had* told me something like that, but I had tuned her out, of course. She became a Christian five years ago, back when I was seventeen. Having my mother suddenly get all religious was one of the most embarrassing things I'd ever experienced.

"Listen here," I whispered, "this skirt is leather and cost me a hundred and twenty-six bucks. I'm not dunking it in any water."

Mama gave my skirt a disbelieving stare. "A hundred and twenty-six bucks for *that*? There ain't enough leather in that skirt to get me a pair of shoes out of!"

I crossed my arms over my chest and put on my most stubborn glare. Mama looked at me for a minute and then sighed.

"Oh, all right. Slip the skirt off. The congregation can only see you from the waist up anyway. And the robe will hide your underwear from Pastor Pa—oh, *Lord have mercy*, Mayla, where in the world did you get those?"

I had dropped the skirt to my ankles, and she stood staring with wide eyes at my cute little hot pink panties. Heat flooded my face. I really hadn't thought I'd be prancing around the church showing them off. But it was pretty obvious that when the white robe got wet, there wouldn't be much hidden beneath it.

"Here," she said, reaching up under her skirt and pulling off her own half-slip, "you'd better wear this under the robe. Pastor Paul is a man of the cloth, but he *is* a man, after all."

Suited up, I turned for Mama's inspection. She'd gone all teary again and sniffed mightily as she looked me up and down.

"Just like an angel," she said in a choked voice.

I couldn't quite imagine an angel in pink panties and purple hair, but I refrained from making that particular comment, since it was a touching moment and all.

Mama opened a door, not the same one we came in, and on the other side I saw the baptismal pool. It looked like a big, deep bathtub, or maybe a small swimming pool. Steps led down into it, and on the other side more steps led up to another door. Pastor Paul stood in the other doorway already, in a white robe of his own. He had taken off his jacket and tie but still wore his white shirt beneath the robe. He stepped down into the water, then smiled and held out his hand to me.

The water felt warm. The robe billowed up as I stepped in, and I hurriedly pushed it down so I wouldn't show anything unladylike to the preacher. He met me in the middle, a matter of a step for each of us, and he put his arm around my shoulders. When he turned me to face outward I saw that we stood up behind the altar in the sanctuary in a little window-type opening, with the whole congregation looking on.

"Mayla Strong," Pastor Paul said in a booming voice, "the sacrament of baptism is a holy one, an outward symbol of the inward change that happens when you accept Jesus Christ into your life. Have you come here of your own free will?"

I fought the urge to look back at Mama, but I could feel her eyes on me from the robe room.

"Yeah, I have," I replied. That was true. No one forced me. There was, of course, about five years worth of begging and crying behind my decision to be here, but no one had twisted my arm.

"And are you prepared to commit your life to Christ, to die and be born again as a new creation of His, to let Him lead you wherever He will and never turn your back on Him?"

Die? I knew that couldn't possibly mean what I thought it meant, but I had certainly never had someone ask me if I was ready to die before. I must have looked a bit shocked, because Pastor Paul's eyes widened and his grip on my shoulder tightened.

"When I say die," he whispered, "it's symbolic. Your old self, your sinful self, dies. We call it 'dying to sin.' Then Jesus gives you a brand new life, one where your sins are forgiven so you can live with Him forever in heaven."

I glanced toward the congregation. They were real quiet out there. Some people leaned forward in their pews, trying to catch what we were saying.

"As long as this dying you're talking about doesn't involve you holding me under this water until I stop breathing," I ventured cautiously, "then I suppose that'd be okay."

The preacher was quiet for a long time. He looked at me like he was trying to see behind my eyeballs, and I got a little antsy under his stare. The people in the congregation shifted in their seats, and a few of them started whispering to one another.

"What?" I finally said, my voice low so no one could hear. "Is something wrong?"

He sighed. "I'm just trying to figure out if you really know what you're doing here. Much as I'd love to baptize you right now, I just can't do that if you don't really know what you're signing up for."

That made sense, and I appreciated his honesty. I heard Mama gasp behind me, though, and I figured she might faint dead away if she finally got me this far only to have the preacher kick me out of the water.

"Well," I said, trying to put the words together into some sort of sense before they came out of my mouth, "to be honest,

I didn't have any idea that I'd be doing this today. But when you were preaching awhile ago I heard you say something that sort of . . . went inside me, if you know what I mean."

I paused, and Pastor Paul nodded encouragingly.

"You were talking about that guy who had been killing Christians and trying to stomp out the church from the face of the earth when Jesus appeared to him in a bright light. And Jesus said to him, 'Why are you hurting me?' And, well, when you said those words, I felt like you were saying them to me."

I stopped for a minute. For some reason I felt like something had lodged in my throat, and I could feel tears coming.

"I mean," I went on in a rush, "I haven't killed anybody or anything like that. But I sure haven't been too nice to church people, my mama included. And then you said Jesus loved that guy, just like He loves us all. And I figured if Jesus could love some guy who went around killing His friends, maybe He really does love me, too. And if He does, then I really am hurting Him, because it hurts to love someone who doesn't love you back."

I heard Mama give a huge sniff behind me.

"If you want to love Jesus," Pastor Paul said, "then there's only one way to do that. You have to turn your life over to Him. You have to let Him be your Lord. That means He's the boss of your life from now on. Can you do that?"

I thought about that. This felt like a real big question, and I didn't want to give a quick answer.

"Does that mean He's going to make me stop running around with my friends?"

Pastor Paul pursed his lips, considering, before he answered.

"I can't tell you what He's going to make you do," he said honestly. "Only that when He changes you, the changes come from the inside out. He might change you so much that you won't want to run around with the same people anymore. Or He might one day use you get through to them, too."

I almost laughed at the thought of Tattoo Lou accepting Jesus, but only for a second. Because in the next second I remembered Lou writhing on the floor, crashing from a bad drug trip and crying over his little sister who had been killed in a gang fight a few years back. I realized that maybe Tattoo Lou needed to know about this love as much as I did.

"Okay," I said, nodding to Pastor Paul. "I understand. I'm ready to let Him be my boss."

"Do you believe that Jesus is the Son of God?"

I had heard that before. "Yes, I do."

"Do you believe that He died on the cross and then rose from the dead and won the power to save you from your sins?"

"Yes, I believe that." Mama had been spouting this stuff at me for a long time. I guess some of it had sunk in.

"And do you accept Jesus as *your* personal Lord and Savior?"

Here was the big moment. I paused, and I admit it was a little bit for effect. I could almost hear Mama's sweat dripping on the floor in the robe room behind me.

"Yes, I do accept Jesus as my personal Lord and Savior."

"Then let's pray. Repeat what I say, but say it to the Lord."

He bowed his head and closed his eyes. I sneaked a quick peek into the congregation, and most of them had bowed their heads, too. Closing my eyes, I tried to picture myself talking to God. His face wasn't clear, but I figured that didn't matter. He knew I was talking to Him.

"Dear Lord, I confess that I'm a sinner."

The preacher's voice sounded reverent when he prayed, and I tried to make mine sound the same.

"Dear Lord, I confess that I'm a sinner." Wouldn't my friends be shocked to hear me say that?

"And I know I can never be good enough to deserve the eternal life You died to give me."

The lump returned to my throat, and I had to swallow a few times before I could repeat that one. "I can never be good enough to deserve the life You died to give me."

Pastor Paul's hand gave my shoulder a gentle squeeze. "So I give You my life, Lord. I ask You to come into my heart and make me into the person You want me to be."

My eyes were shut, but that didn't stop a tear from slipping between my lids and sliding down my cheek as I spoke. "Jesus, I give You my life. Come into my heart and make me into the person You want me to be."

Pastor Paul's voice boomed, "Amen!" I opened my eyes to see him grinning down at me. "Mayla Strong, I baptize you in the name of the Father, and of the Son, and of the Holy Ghost."

He cupped my hand in his, and then he placed both our hands over my nose and mouth. I pinched my nose shut, because I never have been too good at going underwater. His other hand slid down to the middle of my back, and then he gently pushed me backward. I tensed for a moment, but then leaned back on his arm and the next thing I knew I was under the water, face-up.

A second later, Pastor Paul stood me up again. I came up dripping, of course, but I barely noticed. It was strange, but I had this feeling inside, a warm sort of feeling. It's hard to describe, but I felt . . . clean. Like I'd been scrubbed with a bristle brush, then rinsed and wrapped in a warm, fluffy towel and hugged tight. Only it was an inside sort of clean. I knew, right then, that I was different. Changed. And life would never be the same again.

✝

I said that I'm grateful to the Lord for Pastor Paul. But someone else who's high on my list is my mama.

Some people think it's strange that a grown woman still uses the name Mama, but that's only people who don't come from the South. Kentucky *is* part of the South, though some folks argue about that. It's not Scarlett O'Hara's South, but in many ways the society in Kentucky is just as southern as Atlanta's, especially in the small towns. Salliesburg is about as small as they come and still get to have a post office.

Mama fit in that town like a rich bachelor fits in a red sports car. She worked at the Bundle-O-Savings grocery store as a checker, and just about everyone in town came through there at least once a week. Mama never met a stranger, and anyone who went through her checkout aisle didn't walk away without knowing everything there was to know about her and me and everyone else she knew. Not that she gossiped, really; she spoke so openly about her own life that she made it impossible to be offended. She never told people's secrets, as long as she knew they were supposed to be kept secret. But if someone found out they were going to have a baby or were getting ready to put their house on the market, Mama could be counted on to spread the news. I guessed people just didn't tell Mama anything they didn't want announced to all of Salliesburg. Of course, I didn't have that option.

Anyway, when I was growing up, before Mama found the Lord and claimed her place in His kingdom, she tried just about everything out there in the way of religion. For a while, she believed in reincarnation. She was convinced she had been a Chinese man in her last life and some sort of Egyptian priestess in the one before. Another time, she was into witchcraft. Nobody knew anything about Wiccans back then, but there were books to teach you how to cast spells and things like that. I have a vivid memory of Mama sitting at the kitchen table, staring for hours at a deep-green juice glass that stubbornly refused to levitate.

I remember another time, when I was eleven, after Daddy died. I got out of bed late at night to find that Mama wasn't in the house. I had a few moments of pure panic, racing from room to room, so scared I couldn't force any sound out of my mouth, even a sob. I found her outside, lying in the front yard just staring up at the stars in the sky. I stood in the doorway until my heart stopped pounding and then joined her. I can still feel the grass, cold and slightly damp through my thin cotton nightgown. Mama didn't look at me, but after a while she said, "There are people out there."

I considered that for a moment.

"What kind of people?"

"Aliens," Mama answered without hesitation. "People from other planets. They live on worlds like ours, with grass and trees and water, and they're doing their best to find us, just like we're trying to find them."

I remember those stars and an overwhelming awe that different kinds of people might live out there among them. I didn't wonder why Mama thought things like that, and I never questioned whether or not other people thought the same things. She was my mama, and her word was enough for me.

When I think about it now, I realize how much Mama and I were alike in our searching days. We were both looking for something to lift us out of the mundane routines of life, to show us the meaning beyond just living and breathing and getting dressed in the morning. Mama had one up on me; she somehow seemed to know that her questions wanted a spiritual answer. I figured, as usual, that I could do it my own way.

My own way included decorating my body in a manner sure to draw attention. I started out by piercing my ears, of course, and had four holes on each side plus the cartilage on one. Then, when I turned twenty-one, I celebrated by piercing my nostril, and I liked that so much that the next year I got a labret stud too, a silver ball centered a half-inch below my mouth.

If I'm honest with myself—and I make it a policy to try to be honest with myself, if no one else—facial piercing was my way of thumbing my nose at people once I had their eyes fixed on me. I don't know why other people pierce their bodies; I only know why I did it. I enjoyed the way people looked at me, even when those looks were somewhat horrified or disgusted. If they glared or said rude things to me, I felt satisfied somehow, like they were only acting as I had known they would all along. The funny thing is, I didn't much care *what* they thought of me, as long as they thought of me. It was, like, "Hey, I'm here and I make a difference. I'll have an impact, even if it's only to make you swear you'll never pierce your nose."

Back to being grateful for Mama. Because Mama spent a big chunk of time trying to find something to give her life meaning, she always had a lot of tolerance for those still trying to figure it out. That was never clearer to me than the day of my baptism into the kingdom of heaven.

She took me home and called every one of her friends to spread the good news, and to invite them over for a big celebration dinner that evening. I heard her on the phone, telling the story over and over of how I was baptized in pink "hooker" panties and a tiger-print blouse. Even I had a hard time with being compared to a hooker, but she ignored my protests. After the third call, I gave up trying to stop her. It does no good to get embarrassed about anything in Salliesburg. Everybody knows everything about everyone anyway, and I've been the subject of the town gossip line more times than I care to count.

After she'd made the last call, she turned to me and gave me That Look.

I had come to recognize That Look over the years. It preceded a statement that Mama knew was going to cause a ruckus. Her lips got tight, not frowning but not smiling either, and her deep brown eyes opened just a little wider than normal. The crease at the very top of her nose between her unplucked eyebrows deepened. I could always judge Mama's mood by how deep that crease got. Her nostrils sort of flared as she took a deep breath, and her chin jutted out.

"Now that you're a Christian," she said, speaking in a precise tone, "it's time to think about takin' that jewelry out of your face and maybe dyin' your hair back to its normal color."

I wasn't surprised. The nostril ring hadn't seemed to bother her much, but when I came home with the labret stud, her eyes had popped a bit. We'd had several "discussions" about it, which mostly ended with me saying, "Because I want it, and that's that!" This time I surprised myself. Instead of getting defensive, I felt genuinely concerned. This Christianity stuff was new to me, and I didn't want to do anything wrong so soon.

"You don't think Christians wear labret studs?"

"I do not," she replied with a firm shake of her head.

"But you wear jewelry."

Now you'll think I was being argumentative. I wasn't. I truly did not see the difference. Jewelry is jewelry, after all. True, I display mine more prominently than she does, but it's still jewelry.

"It's not the same," Mama said.

"And you dye your hair."

Mama's hand went to pat her auburn curls, which didn't move under the ton of hairspray she used every morning to cement them into place. "Only to color the gray, you know that."

I snorted. "Your hair was brown before it turned gray. That's not your normal color."

"That is entirely different," she insisted. "Auburn is a normal hair color. Purple is not."

"First of all," I told her, "my hair is not purple. It's Egyptian Plum. And second, old Mrs. McCoy has blue hair, and her sister Mrs. Watson has pink hair."

"Those are rinses they use to brighten up their dull gray. Besides, they're in their eighties. They can have any color hair they want."

"So can I."

"Mayla, what will people think? You want people to know you're a Christian, don't you? People won't know you're a Christian if you look like you just robbed the 7-Eleven."

I was still thinking about that when the doorbell chimed, and the first of our guests arrived.

By four o'clock, Mama's little house had filled to bursting with fellow children of God wanting to welcome me into the kingdom with a plate of fried chicken or a Jell-O salad. Mama had put a cheery sunflower-covered tablecloth on the dining room table, and in no time at all the surface was covered with casseroles and salads and trays of sandwiches and carrot sticks with dip.

The old ladies in support hose and sturdy shoes claimed the living room. There must have been a dozen or so in there, enthroned on Mama's old davenport and straight-backed chairs, with white foam plates balanced carefully on their knees and napkins properly covering their laps as they forked delicate amounts of potato salad and baked beans into their mouths. Mrs. McCoy and Mrs. Watson sat side by side, squashed into a big armchair near the window. Mrs. McCoy wore a wide-brimmed straw hat covered with pink and blue flowers. As I watched, she turned her head to speak to an old lady I didn't know, and when she did, the brim of her hat hit her sister squarely in the nose. It so startled Mrs. Watson that she jumped, and the cube of red Jell-O on her fork went flying into the air and landed right in the middle of the flowers on her sister's hat. Mrs. Watson stared at it for a moment, dumbfounded. She raised her fork in the air as if prepared to go after it, and then changed her mind. Her eye caught mine, and she grinned and shrugged. I left the room, chuckling.

The men had taken themselves and their food outside to the covered porch, where they could sit around and watch the trees grow in silence without having to worry about responding to their wives' constant, "Isn't that right, dear?" They could not have asked for a nicer day to sit outside. Mid-May in Kentucky is beautiful when it's not raining, and that day the sky was clear. It wasn't hot enough for the humidity to be oppressive, and yet the sun shone overhead in a bright blue sky, and the icy chill of the hard winter just past seemed a far distant thing. Jonquils had bloomed all over Mama's yard, and the sunlight made their yellow blossoms glow like little spots of fire in the green grass.

"How is everyone doing out here?" I asked, stepping through the screen door.

"Oh, hmmm," muttered someone from the vicinity of the porch swing.

Two men had the swing, two more sat in chairs on either side of the swing, and about a half-dozen more were on a circle of metal folding chairs out under the big oak tree in the front yard. Most were old, but I saw a few unlucky middle-aged men who had been dragged along to the celebration by their wives on this gorgeous day. Either that or they came for the food, which they all socked away as fast as they could shovel it in.

"Can I get anybody anything?" I asked. "Something to drink, maybe?"

No one answered, but a couple of them shook their heads. I stood there a minute, staring out at the group under the tree. Older men often didn't know how to react to a young person like me. It's as if facial jewelry startles them so that they forget there's a person behind it. I thought about what Mama had said earlier. Would people refuse to accept me as a Christian because of my labret stud or my nostril ring? If I couldn't get them to talk to me, I supposed I'd never have a chance to find out.

I had never tried much to talk to anyone who didn't approach me first. Before that morning, if I asked a question and got no response, I probably would have turned and left. But now I wanted to see something. I wanted to see if I could get one of them to talk to me like I was a normal person, nose ring or not.

The man standing closest to me was Mr. Grierson, the owner of the Salliesburg Hardware Store. I had known Mr. Grierson casually since Mama and I moved to town four years ago, when I had gone into his store in a panicked search for a toilet plunger. Mr. Grierson sat on Mama's porch rocker, holding a plate piled high with food beneath his chin, a paper napkin shoved down in the neck of his plaid cotton shirt. As he scooped an impressive amount of coleslaw onto his fork and shoved it in his mouth, I asked, with the perfect timing of waitresses everywhere, "So, Mr. Grierson, how long have you been a Christian?"

He stopped chewing, as if his jaw had been flash-frozen, the empty fork poised in midair an inch from his lips. The look he turned upon me held a hint of alarm.

"Huh?" he said around the coleslaw.

"I mean, were you baptized as a kid, or after you grew up?"

His left eyelid began a nervous twitch as he gave a few quick chews and swallowed with a gulp. "Uh, a kid."

I smiled, hoping it would put him at ease. "Oh, you're lucky then. You grew up knowing how to act and all. I'm going to have to start now, and you know what they say: It's much easier to learn something the right way than to unlearn the wrong way before you finally get it right."

"Hmmm."

He nodded, his eyes casting wildly around as if looking for the cavalry to come riding into view.

His rescue came. From the swing, old Mr. Colvin, deaf as a broom handle and with a face like an old potato, waved his plastic fork in my direction, clutching a chicken leg in his other hand.

"Wanna know when I was baptized?" he asked, his voice loud despite his fragile appearance. I wondered if he needed to change the batteries in his hearing aid.

"Yes, sir," I shouted back at him, turning my attention from poor Mr. Grierson.

"Nineteen thirty-eight it was. I was twenty-five years old, an' it was right down there in the Kentucky River." He shook his fork at me for emphasis. "None of this nonsense about chlorine, or testin' the water then. We went right on down to the river, dirt an' fish an' all, an' we took care of business just like the Lord back in Bible times."

"That must have been exciting."

"Pshaw!" he scoffed, his bushy gray eyebrows dropping right

down onto his eyelids, "Exciting, nothing! It was dad-blamed cold, that's what it was!"

With that he shoved the half-gnawed chicken leg between his wrinkled lips and turned away. Thus dismissed, I headed for the house.

As I reached for the screen door, I caught sight of a man standing off to one side of the porch, away from the others. I had never seen him before. Though not as old as Mr. Colvin, this man had at least a decade or two on the rest of the guys hanging around outside. Judging by his wrinkled skin and sparse, gray hair, I guessed his age at somewhere around seventy-five. A tall man with shoulders slightly stooped beneath dingy red suspenders, he leaned against the side of the house, an empty plate resting between the wooden porch rails in front of him. His gaze locked on to mine for a second. I saw his eyes lift to my hair, then drop to my labret stud before he turned away with tight lips, shaking his head slowly.

I got that reaction a lot. Shrugging off a wave of irritation, I went inside.

The kitchen was full of middle-aged women fussing around with pitchers and ice and lemonade mix.

"Mayla, darling," crooned Olivia Elswick, a lady from Mama's Tuesday night ladies' group, "we're so pleased for you."

She patted me on the shoulder, and I smiled at her while I filled a little paper cup with ice from a bag in the freezer.

"Now then, when are you going to take those things out of your face?"

My smile froze, and I turned toward her. From across the room I locked eyes with Mama, who gave a little warning shake of her head.

"Oh, I can't do that," I told Mrs. Elswick matter-of-factly, "or the holes will close up. You have no idea what I went through to have them done."

Her lips were outlined with brick-red lip liner, and between the lines her lipstick had dulled so that they looked like the outlines in a coloring book for kindergarten kids.

"Surely as a Christian you won't be wearing them anymore." She smiled, as if speaking to a child, and actually patted my arm. "I mean, it's just not something a Christian does."

"Oh?" I resisted the temptation to wipe my arm with my napkin. "And why not?"

"Well . . ." She looked flustered. "Because it just isn't. It's not *normal*, you know."

The other conversations in the room stopped as everyone waited to hear how I would respond. Mama seemed frozen at the other end of the kitchen, a warning not to say anything embarrassing written all over her face.

"That depends on where you are," I answered. "At some bars I know in Lexington, you'd be the one who didn't look normal, not me."

"Ah." Her smile became condescending. "But I wouldn't go to those bars. And neither should you, now that you're a Christian."

This was the first evidence I'd had that a change had taken place in me. Just a few hours before, I would have gotten angry if anyone had told me I *shouldn't* do something. I knew that's what Mama thought was happening right now, that I was getting mad as a hornet and ready to lay into Mrs. Elswick. Instead I filled my cup with lemonade from a jar with a little spigot and took a gulp before I spoke again.

"I guess I'll have to be looking for a new job then, huh, Mrs. Elswick? I mean, I work in a restaurant with a bar. I serve drinks to people. Surely Christians shouldn't be seen in restaurants where they have liquor, should they?"

"Now," she began, her finger pointing at me, "I never said—"

"No," I interrupted with a smile, "you didn't. Because I've seen you in my restaurant, haven't I, Mrs. Elswick? I've even served you wine, haven't I?"

A few chuckles sounded around the room while Mrs. Elswick's face took on a shade of red that clashed terribly with her pink blouse. She opened her mouth to say something, and judging by her expression it would not have been nice. Mama stopped her. She crossed the room and put her arm around my shoulders, giving me a squeeze.

"You know, Olivia, Mayla and I had this very same conversation just this afternoon. And I've been thinking about it." She smiled. "The Lord Himself welcomed tax collectors and prostitutes into His fellowship. The Good Book doesn't say He made them change their clothes first, or take a bath or anything. It just said He loved them. And I know He loves Mayla just as she is, pierced lip, nostril, and all. I reckon that jewelry and that hair went under the water this morning along with the rest of her. So we don't know, maybe the Lord has plans for those things, just like He has plans for Mayla."

Mama squeezed me around the shoulders again, and she smiled at me. Sometimes when my mama smiles, it's like the Lord Himself is peeking out of her eyes.

Chapter 2

The "Welcome to the Kingdom" potluck was winding down when Pastor Paul finally arrived. I saw him through the living room window as he parked his Ford Escort on the grass in Mama's front yard and walked up to the group of men under the tree. They got up out of their chairs, and he shook hands all around, then stood and talked to them a few minutes. Beside me, old Mrs. Watkins saw him too and hollered into the kitchen with a volume I wouldn't have thought her frail old body could produce.

"Oh Angela, the preacher's just come. I hope there's some food left for him."

There was, but the casseroles were starting to look picked over. Mama came rushing out of the kitchen toward the front door, followed by a whole flock of women, just in time to pounce on him as he walked into the house.

"Come right on in," Mama told him. "Grab a plate and help yourself."

"Oh, Pastor Paul," Mrs. Elswick gushed, taking his arm and guiding him to the table, "you're just in time. We've been talking about the choir's program for the Fourth of July. Don't you think the songs should all have a religious element instead of including just any old patriotic thing?"

I watched as the preacher smiled at her and extracted his arm from her clutch to pick up a plate.

"Since I have no musical ability at all," he told her as he eyed the food, "I'm comfortable leaving that up to Ted. That's why he's the choir director, and I'm just a humble servant of God."

Mrs. Davis, the choir director's wife, turned away with a smirk, and Mrs. Elswick's face fell as she realized she couldn't recruit the preacher to aid her in her cause to keep "Yankee Doodle Dandy" off the program. That didn't stop her from following him around the table like a shadow, insisting that he take a huge helping of her green bean casserole while she dished up extravagant compliments about his sermon that morning. Mama caught my eye, the edges of her lips twitching with suppressed laughter as we watched Pastor Paul gently handle the shameless attempt at flirtation.

It must be hard, I realized, being a young pastor in a small-town church. He couldn't be much past thirty, and I guessed the people of Salliesburg Independent Christian Church weren't easy to win over. I seemed to remember Mama telling me when they hired him a few years back that they weren't sure a man that young, and single, could handle the job. As I watched him joke with the women while they all tried to wait on him, and as I saw the way the men treated him with respect, I realized he had done it. I doubted I would ever be accepted by those people the way he had been. Of course, he didn't have purple hair, which probably helped his cause a lot.

As I turned back toward the living room, I glanced through the window and caught sight of the older man I had seen earlier out on the porch. He had moved over to the circle of chairs under the tree and now stood on the edge of the group, hands stuffed in the pockets of his baggy jeans, listening to the lazy conversation of the rest of the men. Odd, him standing there like that, just listening.

"Hey, Mama," I said, calling her over with a nod of my head toward the window. "Who's that man out there, the one with the suspenders?"

Mama squinted in his direction. "Oh, that's Mr. Holmes. He does janitorial work at the church. Didn't you get introduced?"

I shook my head. "No, but that's okay. He didn't look like he wanted to meet me anyway."

She patted my arm as she turned to join the rest of the ladies clustered around the preacher. "Don't mind him. His wife died years ago, and he's had a rough life. He can be a grouch, but he's all right."

I stood watching him a moment longer. He looked sad, standing there apart from the rest of the men, just watching and not joining in. Kind of like a loner who didn't belong. I knew how he felt.

As I picked up a blue plastic Wal-Mart bag full of leftovers and got ready to drive back to my apartment in Lexington, the preacher took me off to the side and gave me a present.

A Bible.

Now, I already had a Bible. Somewhere. Mama gave it to me for Christmas a few years back, and as far as I knew the pages had never even been exposed to air. I wasn't real sure where I had put it, but I'd been thinking about it off and on all afternoon, figuring that now would be a good time to get it out. I thought it might be in a box of junk in the back of my closet, under my high school yearbooks and the mini Crock-Pot I hadn't the faintest idea what to do with that someone gave me for graduation. I had planned to pull that box out and go through it that very night. Pastor Paul's gift saved me the trouble.

"This is just what I need," I told him.

Pastor Paul nodded, his face serious. "It is what you need, Mayla. Take my advice and read a little every day. It takes practice to learn to 'lean on the Everlasting Arms,' so you want to develop good habits right from the first."

Since I had never practiced any sort of leaning, this was all new to me. "So where do I start?"

"I always suggest the book of Luke as a starting place. And don't forget to pray."

"Pray?"

"Pray," he repeated with a firm nod. "See, I've marked a page for you. It says, 'Pray continually; give thanks in all circumstances, for this is God's will for you in Christ Jesus.' You do that, and you'll be just fine."

"I don't know any prayers," I told him, fanning through the pages. "Are there any good ones in here you recommend?"

Pastor Paul smiled, shaking his head. "You don't need a prayer that somebody else wrote, Mayla. Just talk to God. That's all prayer is anyway. He would much rather you tell him what's on your mind than to hear you recite something."

I thanked him, and promised I would do as he said.

I started that very hour, in the car. I really didn't know how to go about this prayer business, but I have always been pretty good at talking, as long as there was someone I wanted to talk to. And I did want to talk to God.

"Uh, hello God," I said as I pulled from Main Street onto Highway 421 heading toward Lexington. "How You doin' up there?"

There was, of course, no answer. I felt awkward and sort of foolish, but that was okay. I wasn't worried about feeling foolish. Determined to do this thing right, I kept going.

"Things down here are just fine, as You probably already know. And I would like to thank You for everything that happened today. I've never felt anything like that feeling I had when I came up out of the water, but it sure did help to feel it. Made me know that something really happened down there, You know?

"Anyway, I guess I'd just like to say that I'm planning on reading the Bible like Pastor Paul told me, and I'm going to pray every day. And I sure would appreciate it every now and then if You'd let me know how I'm doing. I'm new at this, as You know, so if I do anything wrong just tell me, and I'll try not to do it again."

I paused, waiting for . . . something. I didn't know what, but I expected some sort of answer, a sign maybe. Like a shooting star, or a bright light, or an angel.

"Well," I went on, after giving the Almighty sufficient time to respond, "I guess that's all. Thanks for listening. I'll talk to You again later, okay? Good-bye. Uh, Amen."

Something did happen then. Nothing dramatic like stars or lights or angels, only a feeling. At first I thought maybe I was just tired and trying too hard to hear from the Lord, but then I wasn't so sure. I had the oddest feeling suddenly, like

someone had joined me there in the car, sitting closer to me
than the passenger seat, and that He was laughing. Not laughing *at* me, particularly, but laughing because He was so pleased.
It does seem sort of pompous to think I could do anything that
would make the Lord laugh, but it made me feel good anyway.
I laughed along with Him, right out loud.

I figured that probably wouldn't be the last time I gave the
Lord a good laugh, and that was okay with me.

I shared an apartment with a girl named Sylvia Thomas.
Once I nicknamed her Sly, like Sylvester Stallone, and teased
her that she looked just like Rambo. That wasn't true, of course.
She has been known to *act* like Rambo, but she didn't look anything like him. A tiny little thing, she stood a good four inches
shorter than my five-five, and she was so skinny she had to
shop for clothes in the children's department. She wore underwear with the Little Mermaid on them.

As a bartender at The Max, Sylvia had gotten me a night
job waiting tables. She made enough money that she didn't
work days, but I had to have a daytime job, too. I worked as a
receptionist for a small construction company. As a server, I
made good money in tips on weekend nights, but the day job
paid my rent.

Anyway, when I got home that Sunday night, Sylvia had
already left for work. I waited up for her, curled on the couch,
thumbing through my new Bible to get familiar with it. Pastor Paul had given me a nice one, a study Bible with notes at
the bottom of every page explaining things about the verses
up above. At the beginning of every book was a description of
who wrote it, and when and why. I felt grateful to Pastor Paul

all over again, because those little notes helped. I spent awhile getting to know the author of the book the preacher had recommended, Luke, and then plunged right in.

To my surprise, I found myself captivated by what I read. Always before when I tried to read the Bible—like when Mama forced me to at Christmas before she'd let me open my presents—I couldn't concentrate. It was like trying to read a foreign language; all those *thees* and *thous* and *begats* seemed to get in the way of the story, and I wasn't interested enough to try to see around them. This time the words built pictures in my mind like a television set. I read about Zechariah and Elizabeth and how their son was born, and I could picture them. I felt like I knew what they looked like. When they circumcised their baby boy and Zechariah started speaking again, I got goose bumps!

I read far into the night, devouring the entire book of Luke. I couldn't put it down. The Lord Jesus just jumped right out of the pages at me, and when He talked, I felt as if He spoke right to me. I cried when He was murdered, and when the apostles saw Him being taken up into heaven, I cheered out loud. Right out loud. A big "Yahoo!" so loud it startled me.

I looked at the clock. One a.m. The restaurant closed at ten on Sunday nights, so Sylvia must have gone to a party somewhere. I sighed. I wanted to tell her what had happened to me that day, but my news would have to wait.

As I slipped between the sheets in my bed, I said another quick prayer.

"That was pretty good writing, Lord. If You happen to run into ol' Luke up there, You can tell him I said so. Good night."

The construction business has its good times and its bad times. If the weather is bad, construction slows to a halt and no one makes any money. But in good weather business booms, and the weather had been good for a couple of weeks. At Clark and Hasna Building Company, we had broken ground on several new sites and were hiring people like crazy. Orders were placed for concrete and tie wire and wallboard and studs. Those same orders were delivered to the wrong sites and had to be tracked down and transported, and half the workers never showed up on Mondays. I was so busy I hardly had time to go to the bathroom.

The company's office fronted the warehouse where we stored equipment and excess material. I sat behind a high counter facing the front door and the big plate glass windows with the company name painted on them. My desk stayed in a state of constant clutter, with piles of invoices and file folders and sticky notes reminding me of a million things I didn't want to forget. I had a telephone, a big calculator, a computer, and a grimy-looking laser printer. My official title was receptionist, but I did a lot more than that. Besides answering the phone, I handled all the orders, paid all the invoices, kept the bank ledger up to date, and did anything else the bosses gave me to do. I had started working there when I was nineteen, and I knew almost everything there was to know about running the office.

Behind me, and in front of the two doors leading to the bosses' tiny offices, was a much neater desk that belonged to Alison Harper, the company's secretary. Alison's responsibilities included typing letters and making appointments for Mr. Clark and Mr. Hasna. And filing her nails, which is how she spent most of her time.

A few minutes before lunchtime, Alison walked over and sat on the corner of my desk. I didn't have a problem with Alison, but we didn't talk much. She was older than me,

probably close to thirty, and had perfect blonde hair and polished fingernails. She wore coordinated skirts and blouses, and
wouldn't have been caught dead going on a job site because
she might get mud on her matching high-heeled shoes. I never
thought Alison liked me. She always treated me nicely, but I'd
caught her several times looking down her nose at my hair or
my jeans. So I tended to ignore her most of the time.

"Okay," she said, perching on the edge of my desk, "what
gives?"

I looked up from the stack of mail I was opening. "Huh?"

"What gives?" She spoke slowly, as if to a child. "I want to
know what happened to you."

Was I wearing a sign? "What do you mean?"

"I've been watching you all morning. You've been running
like a crazy woman, yet you haven't cussed once. Not once.
That's just not you. Last week, if Sutherland's had delivered
that wallboard order to the wrong site, you would have blistered
Pat's ears, but all you said was, 'Oh they're on Lincoln Avenue?
Thanks, I'll send someone for them.' So I want to know what
happened to the Mayla who left here last Friday calling her
boss a mean, nasty so-and-so and saying he should—"

"Okay, I get it," I said hastily, recalling what I had said
about Mr. Clark and not wanting to hear it repeated.

A funny little tickle started in the pit of my stomach. This
was it, my first opportunity to tell someone who knew the "old"
Mayla about the "new" Mayla. What should I say? What if I
blew it?

Before I could say a word, it hit me suddenly that Alison
was right. I had not uttered a single bad word all day! I hadn't
consciously tried not to swear, but the words that came out just
weren't the same words as before. And not only that, but it *had*
been a rough morning, and not once—not *once*—had I felt the

gut-gripping frustration that I would have felt if this day had happened last week.

I laughed, suddenly delighted with the Lord. I had become a brand new person!

"What's so funny?" Alison asked, looking at me like she was wondering if she should call for a straightjacket.

I sat back in my chair and laughed again. "Just that it's true, something did happen to me over the weekend, and I just now realized how big that change was. I got baptized yesterday."

Alison couldn't have looked any more stunned if I had announced that I had given birth to a watermelon.

"Baptized? You mean, like in church?"

I nodded, still grinning like a fool. "I became a Christian, and it seems to have cleaned the bad words right out of me."

She sat there a minute, staring at me with her mouth hanging open. I could tell she wanted to say something but she didn't know what.

"Have you ever been baptized, Alison?" I asked.

Her mouth snapped shut, and she stood up. She walked back to her desk on the other side of the room and sat down, her back to Mr. Clark's closed office door. She looked upset. I sat there trying to figure out what to say when she finally answered me.

"Yeah, a long time ago. But I don't think it took."

She looked at me from across the room, and I couldn't be sure, but I thought her eyes looked a little wet. The last thing I wanted was to have Alison Harper crying at her desk. I figured the best thing to do was shut my mouth right then. But I never have been known to do the best thing.

"I don't know much about all this stuff yet," I said slowly, not looking directly at her, "but it seems to me that if it didn't take the first time, maybe you ought to try it again."

She sat there a long time, and I looked anywhere but at her. Picking up a letter from the pile in front of me, I slit it open with my scissors, pulled out the invoice, stamped it with today's date, and set it on top of the others.

Finally Alison gave a short laugh. "What, you get baptized one day and the next you're trying to convert everyone you see?"

I looked up at her then. She no longer looked ready to cry.

"I'm not trying to convert anyone," I told her truthfully. "I wouldn't even know how to go about it. I was just—"

"Well don't bother trying to convert me." She reached into her bottom drawer and pulled out her purse, then stood up and pushed her chair under her desk. "I went to church as a kid, and that was enough. I sleep in Sunday mornings, and I like it that way. I'm going to lunch now."

"Okay," I said. "Have a good one."

She gave me one more odd look before she left the office. I realized that I had probably never told Alison to "have a good one" before.

"Well, Lord," I said out loud after the door closed behind her, "that didn't go so well, did it? And I gotta say, I didn't feel great talking to her, either. I don't think I want to do that again. But thanks for not letting me swear today. I guess it wouldn't look good for me to be cussing up a blue streak the day after I became a Christian, huh? I appreciate You not letting me make a fool out of myself."

As I got back to the stack of mail in front of me, I wondered if Sylvia would notice the difference in me, too.

She noticed, all right.

When I walked into work at the restaurant that evening, she greeted me with, "What was that *thing* sitting on the kitchen table when I got up this afternoon?"

"Hey, Sly, good to see you," I answered with a grin. "What thing on the table?"

I had probably left the butter out. In the past I had been known to leave dirty laundry lying around the living room or half-eaten sandwiches on my pillow. I'm not exactly the neatest person in the world, whereas Sylvia, most definitely, is.

"It was a Bible," she said in a low voice, glancing around to see if anyone could overhear. "And somebody had opened it, like they had been reading it or something."

I sat down on a bar stool and rested my chin on my hand while she wiped the already clean bar with a damp towel.

"I was reading it. You'll never guess what happened to me yesterday."

Sylvia gave me a look full of alarm, her dark eyes wide and round. "Oh no, she got to you, didn't she?"

"Who, Mama? No. But I went to her church, to get her off my back you know, and this guy was talk—"

"Aha!" She let out a sigh of relief. "A guy! I should have known. I thought there for a minute you'd gone and gotten religious on me. But you were just picking up a guy, right?"

"No, I wasn't picking up a guy. I *did* get religious. Well, sort of. I got baptized."

I beamed. Sylvia, however, definitely did not beam. She looked like she had just come upon a snake on the sidewalk and was trying to figure out whether to run or to whack it with a shovel.

"You gotta be kidding me," she said finally. "Please tell me you're kidding."

This conversation was not going as planned. I thought she'd be happy for me.

"The guy," I told her, serious now, "is a preacher. He was talking about this other guy named Paul from the Bible, and how Paul went around killing Christians until Jesus appeared to him and made this big bright light shine in his eyes and he went blind. But only for a little while. And then he—"

"Stop!" Sylvia held up a slender hand. "I don't want to hear it. I don't want you to start lecturing me about anything, either." She leaned across the bar until her face hovered just inches away from mine and whispered. "You're my friend, so I hope this is just something you're going through. Maybe you'll come to your senses and get over it. Until then, you'd better leave me alone. Don't you dare start telling me I shouldn't be partying or letting guys spend the night. If there's anything I can't stand it's a religious nut, and I won't live with one. You understand me, Mayla?"

I nodded, too stunned to speak.

She turned away from me, swiping viciously at the shining bar top. Her mouth, usually so pretty and sweet, clamped into a hard line, and her jaw clenched and unclenched. I climbed down off the bar stool and went back to the server's alley to clock in.

Chapter 3

I opened my apartment door Friday evening just as the phone started ringing. I didn't need Caller ID to know who was on the other end. Mama knew exactly what time I got home from my day job. Grabbing the cordless in the living room, I punched the Talk button as I walked down the hallway toward my bedroom.

"Hey Mama, what's up?"

"Hello baby, did you have a good day at work?"

I had to smile. She always began that way. "It was okay. How 'bout you?"

"Fine. Listen, I'm having some people over for Sunday dinner after church, and I need a count. You are comin' to church, aren't you?"

I dropped my keys on the bed and kicked my shoes into the corner. "Yeah, I'm planning to come down late Saturday night, but I'm leaving right after church 'cause I've got to work. So don't count on me for dinner. I thought I might go to Sunday school with you, though."

"Really?" That surprised her. I could almost hear the smile in her voice. "You're gonna love my class. I learn somethin' new every week."

"Well that's just what I need."

"So, what did the rest of your friends think of your news?"

I had told her about Alison's and Sylvia's reactions, and how they had made me nervous to talk to anyone else.

"I haven't seen anyone," I said. "But there's a party tonight, so I guess I'll find out soon."

Mama paused a long time, and I had a feeling if I could see her face I'd see that crease as deep as the Grand Canyon.

"I don't think you ought to be partyin' now that you're a Christian."

She sounded ready for a fight. If so, I wasn't going to give her one.

"Actually, I've been wondering about that myself," I told her, dropping onto the bed and plumping my pillows against the headboard so I'd have something to lean on. "I don't plan to do any partying myself, but I do want to go. How else will everyone get to know the new Mayla?"

"Hmmm. I think you ought to pray about this, and maybe even ask Pastor Paul."

I sat straight up, suddenly ready to give her that fight. "Why should I ask Pastor Paul? I don't need his permission or anyone else's to hang out with my friends."

"Oh, calm down, Mayla, that's not what I meant. He's a preacher. It's his job to counsel the folks in his church whenever they have questions about their walk with the Lord. That's what he does. You could just give him a call, and he can pray with you. Lots of us do. Olivia Elswick has him programmed into her speed-dial."

Remembering the way Mrs. Elswick had latched on to him at the potluck last weekend, that didn't surprise me. I certainly didn't want to follow in Mrs. Elswick's shoes. On the other hand, I needed an objective opinion. Mama sure couldn't give me that.

"Well, maybe I'll call him."

That made Mama happy. "You do that, baby. Here's his number right here. Got a pencil?"

I fished a pen out of my nightstand and wrote the number she gave me on the back of an old bank statement envelope.

"You pray about it, too," she told me. "I'm sure you'll make the right decision. See you tomorrow night?"

"Okay. Love you, Mama."

"Love you too, baby. Bye."

I sat staring at the number and wondering if I should call him.

"Hey Lord," I said toward the ceiling, which was the general direction where I had always considered heaven to be, "what do You think about this party tonight? Should I go?"

The silence in my room held no answer. I waited a minute, then said, "Oh, what the heck."

I dialed the number. While it rang, I hopped off the bed and went into the kitchen to make myself a sandwich.

"Hello?"

"Pastor Paul?" I cleared my throat.

"Yes, who is this?"

"It's Mayla Strong."

His voice became friendly. "Hello, Mayla! It's good to hear from you. Are you in town?"

"No, I'm in Lexington." I shifted the phone to my left shoulder so I could hold the bread while I spread peanut butter on it.

"Are you reading your Bible every day like we talked about?"

"I sure am. I read Luke, like you said, and then I decided I had gone through it too fast, so I started over. I'm almost finished with it the second time through. Then I figured I would start at the beginning and read Genesis."

"That's good," he said, "but can I make a suggestion?"

"Sure."

"After Luke, read Acts. The same person wrote both books, so Acts sort of picks up where Luke leaves off. Then you might read the Gospel of John, which is one of my favorites. Genesis is a good place to start out in the Old Testament, of course, and you'll find it interesting. Not only are there some wonderful role models for us there, but also some pretty good examples of mistakes we don't want to make. At times you'll think you're reading a supermarket tabloid."

"Okay, that's what I'll do. Thanks. Listen, what I called about is this: do you think it's okay to go to parties?"

He paused, and when he spoke again, I could hear the caution in his voice. "What sort of parties?"

"Just a bunch of guys, no big deal. Every Friday night a group of us who live in my apartment complex get together at someone's house to party, and I always go. But now, well, I'm not sure what to do."

"When you say you get together to 'party' do you mean you drink?"

"Uh-huh."

"And are there drugs?"

I hesitated, but saw no sense in lying. The urge to lie seemed to have gone the way of the cuss words lately. I could still do it, but found that I really didn't want to.

"Well, yeah, sometimes."

A much longer pause. I wondered what he was doing over there, and then it occurred to me that he was probably praying for an answer. I spread grape jelly on a second piece of bread and waited. I hoped the Almighty answered him quicker than He answered me.

"Yes, I think it's okay, but—"

"You do?" I couldn't believe it. Mama would choke when I told her.

"I do. Remember what you read in Luke, about the time Jesus went to the tax collector's house for dinner?"

"Yeah."

"Well, tax collectors were the scum of the earth in Jesus' day. They cheated everyone, the people and the government alike, and everyone hated them. There were prostitutes at that dinner, too, the Bible tells us. Jesus took some heat because He hung out with those 'sinners.' But He knew that God loved them just like He loved the ones who went to the temple every Sabbath. Translated to today, that means God loves your friends, even if they drink and do drugs, just as much as He loves your mother or the ladies in her Tuesday night prayer group."

"I don't think many of them would believe that," I told him, thinking of Sylvia.

"The only thing you need to do," he went on, "is make sure you act like Jesus is right there with you. He is, you know, and if you let Him, He'll show you how to act in a way that honors Him but is still uniquely Mayla. If something illegal starts happening, though, that's your cue to leave. You can leave quietly without making a big fuss about it, but leave just the same."

I smiled. "You're pretty cool for a preacher. I know a few people I'd like to introduce you to. Maybe you ought to go with me tonight."

Pastor Paul laughed out loud. "Much as I'd like to go, I've got a finance committee meeting tonight, and I've got to wrestle twenty-five hundred dollars out of Brother Myron for Vacation Bible School when I know darn well he only wants to give me fifteen."

"Good luck, then. I'm planning on driving to Salliesburg for church on Sunday, so I'll see you then."

"Good luck to you, too, Mayla. I look forward to seeing you on Sunday."

I pressed the End button to disconnect the call, smiling. Pastor Paul was a good guy. I really would have loved to introduce him to Sylvia, but given the way she had reacted to the news about my baptism, she would probably throw him out of the apartment the minute I told her who he was. I smashed the two pieces of bread together and bit into my dinner as I walked toward the bedroom to get dressed for my server job.

The parties that my friends had weren't really parties in the sense that Mama would define a party. I mean, whoever's apartment we went to did not plan for weeks like Mama would have, and they didn't have bowls set out with pretzels and snacks. Heck, they didn't even clean the place most of the time. Really we just needed a time to crash and relax at the end of the week. People brought their own beer or whatever else they wanted to drink, and sometimes someone would spring for a few pizzas. Of course, I usually worked five-thirty to eleven on Fridays, so the party was pretty well underway by the time I got there.

This particular Friday night, Sylvia got off at eleven with me, so we got to Jimmy's place together. He lived in the same complex we did, but in a different building. We walked into the apartment—exactly like ours only a lot dirtier—and several people shouted greetings to us. We had a good turnout tonight, probably thirty people, and someone had cranked up the stereo so loud I thought for sure the Bowens downstairs would complain. They always complained, so I figured they must not be home.

Sylvia caught sight of the guy she had been going out with lately sitting on the couch talking to another guy I had seen a few times but didn't know. She went to join him, grabbing a beer out of a cooler on the way. Blue cigarette smoke filled the room, which didn't bother me much except that it made my eyes water. I stood there a minute, blinking, then headed into the kitchen where it was a little quieter.

"There's Mayla!" a female voice shouted as I came through the entrance.

I suddenly found myself supporting the weight of a drunken woman who proceeded to give me a big hug while spilling beer all over my tee shirt.

"Hey, Lisa, how's it going?" I asked, standing her upright and holding on a moment while she steadied herself.

"Awful," Lisa responded, tossing her blonde hair back with an exaggerated shake of her head. "I got fired from the optometrist office today. Fired. Just like that."

She snapped her fingers in my face for emphasis, her full bottom lip stuck out in a pretty pout.

"What did you do to get fired?"

"Slept late again." She sighed. "I can't seem to get going in the mornings until ten o'clock, but they say I have to be there at nine."

Cameron, a construction worker who roomed with a couple of guys down the hall from Jimmy, leaned against the oven door with a bottle of beer in his hand. He laughed and nudged Lisa's shoulder. "Maybe if you'd get to bed at a decent hour you could get up in the morning."

Lisa turned a flirty look his way and smiled. "Three is a decent hour. For some things."

I stepped around Lisa and opened the refrigerator. Inside I found an open carton of Coke and helped myself to one.

"I can talk to Jolene and see if she needs someone at The Max."

"Oh, would you?" She turned an imploring face my way. "Just until I can find something else, you know."

"No problem," I assured her, and left the kitchen, popping the tab on my Coke.

Five people sat on Jimmy's bed, talking in the relative quiet of the bedroom with a wall separating them from the stereo speakers. I peeked in and smiled a greeting.

"Hey, Mayla," said Stuart, one of my neighbors from upstairs. Though we had only met a few months before, when he moved into the apartment above me, Stuart had quickly become one of my favorite people. He tended to like his music loud—which earned a thump on the ceiling with a broom handle—but Sylvia and I quickly discovered that he was a near perfect neighbor. He laughed a lot, gossiped like a teenager, and made friends with everyone he met. Besides, he loved to cook and we loved to eat.

Stuart's roommate, Michael, who was a lot more than just a roommate, sat beside him on the bed, along with some girls from one of the other buildings in our apartment complex. I came in and flopped down alongside them, hugging Stuart and nodding at the others.

"Nice hair," I told Stuart. He wore his hair short and spiky, and had bleached the tips lighter since I saw him last.

He grinned, his gray eyes twinkling as I patted the prickly top of his head. "Thanks. I had it done yesterday."

"I heard a rumor about you," Michael said, scooting toward the other edge of the bed to give me more room as he turned a lopsided grin my way, "but I didn't believe it."

"If it's that I met a handsome millionaire who fell madly in love with me and swept me off my feet and we're leaving in the morning for Tahiti, it's not true."

Heidi, one of the girls, giggled. "If you really do find one, let me have a go at him."

"No," Michael said, ignoring her, "but it's almost as weird. I heard you went and got religion last weekend."

Stuart collapsed onto Michael's shoulder in a fit of laughter, and the girls snickered and shook their heads. I took a drink of my Coke, my mind working pretty fast, trying to figure out what to say. I felt suddenly shy. Not ashamed, exactly, but uneasy. I wasn't sure how to tell them what happened to me without it sounding cheap or fake. I had been so excited a few days ago, but after Sylvia's reaction I didn't know what to expect from the rest of my friends.

"Well, weird or not, that one's true," I finally said.

Shock wiped the laughter right out of all of them. Stuart sat up straight, and the girls stared at me, open-mouthed.

"You're joking," Stuart said, his expression begging me to agree.

I shook my head. "I got baptized in my mama's church on Sunday."

"No kidding?" Becky, a petite brunette, cocked her head and gave me a skeptical stare. "You don't look any different."

I laughed. "What did you expect, I'm gonna grow wings or suddenly sprout a halo out of my head?"

"Well, no, but I guess I figured you wouldn't still be wearing your jewelry."

I shrugged and took another drink of Coke. Michael, looking horrified, stared at me like I was wearing a Halloween mask.

"Are you going to start going to church every Sunday?" he asked.

"Probably, when I'm not working."

Stuart closed his mouth, which had been gaping wide enough for someone to throw a basketball into, and said, "Are you going to quit drinking and partying?"

"Look," said Becky, pointing at my Coke like she'd just discovered gold, "she's not drinking beer."

I resisted the urge to squirm. "C'mon, you guys, it's not like—"

I shut my mouth. I had almost said, "It's not like I'm a different person or anything," but I couldn't say that. I *was* a different person. To deny it would be to deny my new life in Jesus, and I wasn't going to do that.

They all stared, waiting for me to say something. I took a breath and opened my mouth, not at all sure what was going to come out.

"I don't know what all's going to change now that I'm a Christian," I said honestly. "I'm new at this, and I don't have all the answers. Heck, I don't have any of the answers. I do know that I'm going to keep wearing my jewelry because I like it, and I don't see anything wrong with it. Anything illegal, though, is out, even pot."

"Oh, that's a big sacrifice." Michael's tone dripped sarcasm. "Everybody knows you don't like pot. But what about your friends? Are you going to get chummy with those churchy people and then get to be too good for us?"

"Or worse," added Stuart, "are you going to start telling us we're going to hell because we're gay? You know, Mayla, church people hate gays."

I bit my lip. I knew he was right. Some church people, anyway. I could just imagine what Mrs. Elswick would have to say about it, or Brother Damon. What about Pastor Paul? What would he think about Stuart and Michael? And, more importantly, what would Jesus think?

"I don't know about church people," I said suddenly, reaching over to give Stuart a hug, "but I'm not trying to be like other church people. I'm trying to be like Jesus, and He loves everyone, I know that. Even gays."

I nearly bit my tongue in surprise. Where in the world had that come from? And how did I have the nerve to say it out loud?

But my words seemed to calm them all down. Even Michael relaxed enough to ask about my baptism, and before long I had them in stitches describing my mother's face when she was trying to think of a way to save the preacher from the sight of my pink panties. We talked for almost an hour, and there were no more awkward moments, just a group of friends having fun together.

I left the party happier than I had been in several days. God had handled that situation just fine. At least all my friends weren't going to hate me because I had become a Christian. If only I could convince Sylvia, too, that she didn't have anything to be afraid of in the new Mayla.

I woke up Saturday morning thinking about what Becky had said. And Mrs. Elswick. And Mama, even. Was my labret stud really something that a Christian wouldn't wear?

I got out of bed and went into the bathroom, where I studied my reflection. I wore a simple stud, a four-millimeter silver ball with a fourteen-gauge bar. I liked it. It gave me a certain . . . look. I liked to wear dark silver eye shadow and liner with it, and when I put on my leather skirt and vest and teased my hair, I looked sharp.

When I had my labret done, I was dating a guy named Kevin, who had a standing account at Pete's Piercing Palace on Broadway. Kevin had his labret pierced three times, and to dress for parties or concerts he wore spikes. He also had both nipples and his right eyebrow pierced. I went with him when he had his bellybutton done, and the sight of that hollow needle carving through his skin had cured me from any further piercing ideas I might have had. It also cured me of any romantic interest I had in Kevin. For some reason, I could never look at him quite the same way after that.

As I stood there considering my reflection and remembering Kevin's spikes, I suddenly had an idea. I glanced at my watch. Nine-thirty. Plenty of time before I went to work at The Max at eleven.

An hour later, I stepped out of Pete's Piercing Palace and into the bright sunshine of another beautiful spring day in Kentucky. It had rained in the early morning, and the streets of downtown Lexington had been washed clean of dirt and dust. The crisp air smelled good, without a hint of exhaust fumes but full of freshly ground coffee from the cappuccino bar down the street. I walked down the sidewalk toward my car with a springy step. Catching a glimpse of my reflection in a shop window as I passed, I turned to see myself full-on and smiled as the sunlight glinted off my new labret stud.

Now everyone would know that I was a Christian. I wore the evidence displayed on my face for the world to see. There, embedded beneath my lower lip, was a five-millimeter silver cross.

Chapter 4

When outsiders come to Kentucky for a visit, there are a couple of things they always remark on. Their first comment is almost always, "Hey! You do have indoor plumbing!" The entire world is convinced that Kentucky consists of nothing but hillbillies running barefoot through the bluegrass—which is not Crayola blue, by the way—the women pregnant every year, the men with corncob pipes stuck between their teeth and a shotgun slung over one shoulder. Make no mistake—those people do exist. Whenever Kentucky makes the national news, they always manage to find one of them to interview in front of the camera. They pick a hillbilly who drawls in that hick Kentucky accent, and whose two remaining teeth are black. No wonder

the rest of the nation thinks we're backward. It gets on my
nerves.

The second thing outsiders notice, if they stay any time at
all, is the weather. Then they say, "How can you stand it? The
sun hasn't been out in a week!" Well, the answer to that is: you
get used to it. There are a lot of cloudy, overcast days at certain times of the year. But the land in Kentucky is so beautiful
that when the sun does shine over those softly rolling hills, the
sights and smells and feelings are enough to last through all
the cloudy weather to the next sunny day.

That Sunday, one week after my baptism, was one of those
dreary days when the sun was so securely hidden behind a thick
ceiling of gray that for all we knew it might never have gotten
out of bed that morning. I had driven to Salliesburg after work
the night before, so I didn't get to sleep at Mama's house until
on toward one o'clock in the morning. When the alarm clock
went off at eight, I groaned and hugged a pillow over my head.

"Mayla?" Mama's voice was muffled through the feathers.
"Honey, it's time to get up. Sunday school starts at nine-thirty."

For a minute I thought I was a teenager again and Mama
was waking me up to force me to go to church with her.

"Sunday school?" I moaned. "I don't want to go to Sunday
school."

"I thought you did." Mama's voice sounded a little hurt.
"You said last week you wanted to study the Bible with someone
who knows it. Sam Mullins is one of the best Sunday school
teachers at the church, and we're studying the book of Daniel
right now."

Then I remembered where I was, and who I was, and that
I did want to go to Sunday school and learn about Daniel. I
uncovered my head, actually thankful for the lack of sunshine
in my tired eyes, and smiled at Mama, who smiled back.

"That's better," she said. "You get a shower and I'll get breakfast on the table. I'm making your favorite—chocolate chip waffles."

Chocolate chip waffles! My stomach growled in anticipation. Mama had made chocolate chip waffles on every special occasion for as long as I could remember. Just thinking about them gave me the happy feeling that comes when you wake up in the morning and realize it's your birthday or Easter or the first day of summer.

"What's special about today?" I asked, sitting up and putting my feet on the cold hardwood floor.

Mama patted my shoulder. "You're special, and I'm happy you came home to go to church with me."

My mama has a way of making even the gloomiest day seem bright.

I showered, put on a fluffy bathrobe and slippers, and joined Mama in the kitchen. As I sat at the table, the first of the waffles came off the iron. I covered them with Hershey's syrup and took a big, chocolaty bite. Nothing tastes better than chocolate chip waffles with a black coffee chaser. Mama had the radio tuned to a Christian station, and the sounds of a country gospel group filled the kitchen. I devoured three big waffles, savoring the taste of my childhood, and told Mama that they were as good as ever. Which they were.

I didn't mention the music. She seemed to like it, and even hummed along while she poured batter onto the hot waffle iron. Country music has never been a favorite of mine—that's another misconception about Kentuckians, that we all live for country and bluegrass music—and just because I had become a born-again Christian didn't mean my liking for rock music had changed. The radio in my Honda was now permanently tuned to K-LOVE, and I enjoyed flooding the air with positive, encouraging sound waves. I had discovered the Newsboys and Chasing Furies at a Christian bookstore in Lexington. I loved listening to them, but Mama wouldn't have liked any of it.

There was something else Mama didn't like. I saw her staring at me across the table, her eyes wide and look of pure agitation on her face.

"What?" I asked.

"'*What*' is right," she answered. "Specifically, what is that in your lip?"

I touched my new stud. "A cross. I got it yesterday so everyone will know I'm a Christian. You don't like it?"

"No," Mama said firmly, shaking her head, "I don't."

I was confused. "Why not? I thought you'd be pleased."

Mama bit her lip, considering. "I don't know exactly why. I guess it just seems like you're . . . trivializing the cross or something."

That hurt. "I'm not trivializing the cross. I just wanted to wear something that would show people what's happened to me. You wear a cross, and I figured I could too."

Mama's hand went to the cross hanging from a chain around her neck. She fiddled with it a minute, staring at mine. Then she shrugged.

"I guess you're right. I just wish you'd take it out completely, that's all. But I guess if you're going to wear jewelry in your lip, a cross is better than most things."

"I can't take it out completely," I told her. "It's been ten months. The hole would take a long time to close up."

I could almost hear her answer, "Better a hole—" But she didn't say it. Instead, she shrugged again.

"Maybe you're right. I know you'll hear from the Lord on this, Mayla, and that you'll do whatever He wants you to do. Now you'd better get dressed and I'll just rinse these dishes."

At nine-thirty sharp we walked into the church to be greeted by Pastor Paul. He smiled that great big smile when he saw me, and gave us both one of his friendly handshakes. He smelled of a spicy aftershave scent that reminded me sharply of the way my grandpa used to smell before he died. While he crushed my hand, I was struck with how handsome a man Pastor Paul was. His eyes were almost as dark as his hair, and his jaw was squared and strong. He had a straight nose above lips that were not too full and not too thin. His hair was a little shorter than I liked, of course, but I guessed he had to cut it like that or face the disapproval of all the little old ladies in the church. If he'd let it grow just a few inches longer, so it hung a bit over his collar, and if he'd consider growing a mustache—

I jerked myself back to reality. That was a *preacher* I was thinking about! Of *course* he wasn't good-looking. He was a man of God!

"Isn't that right, Mayla?"

Mama and Pastor Paul looked at me expectantly. I stammered something that sounded like an affirmative, and they both gave me an odd look before going back to their conversation.

"So she'll just go with me into my class," Mama said, "and she'll be fine."

"I think that's probably the best class for you at the moment." Pastor Paul smiled at me. "Esther Thompson is teaching the other adult class, and they're studying a book called *Extreme Faith*. It's a good book, don't get me wrong, but the best thing for a new Christian is to study the Bible."

"Yes, sir," I said, still a little flustered.

Pastor Paul started, then grinned. "Don't call me 'sir' Mayla. It makes me feel like an old man. After all, I'm probably not that much older than you."

Someone came in the door behind us, and before Pastor Paul walked away to greet them, he said in a low voice, "I like your cross."

The book of Daniel was fascinating, and Sam Mullins was a good teacher. I caused a stir when I came into the classroom with Mama. Some of the people stared and things grew quiet, but I was used to a lot worse. Sam Mullins was obviously expecting me. Mama must have called ahead and warned him. He stood up and came around the table with his hand outstretched to take mine.

"Mayla Strong, welcome to our class. Everyone, this is Angela's daughter, Mayla, who was baptized last week. She's going to be coming to our class whenever she's in town."

The people seated in the room nodded, and a few murmured a quiet welcome. Tables had been pushed together to form a big square, and people sat around the outsides facing the front of the room where Sam sat. Mama led me toward two empty chairs, two of the last. The class was pretty full.

The lesson was a good one, too. We all took turns reading from the Bible, and then Sam talked about Daniel's friends, three guys who were thrown into a big furnace because they wouldn't bow down to the god that the king had made. The king tried real hard to scare them into worshiping his false god, but they refused. They weren't worried, because they knew their God, the real one, would take care of them. Sure enough, He saved them, and they didn't get burned up, and they never even got the smell of smoke on their clothes.

Then Sam asked if we wasted time and energy worrying about things when we should be trusting God. It was a profound question, and one I knew I would think about all week. He said that we should be as sure as those three guys were that God will take care of us.

When Sunday school ended, the church suddenly filled with people. Mama and I fought our way up a crowded set of stairs toward the sanctuary, feeling like salmon struggling upstream against an onslaught of parents with small kids heading to the nursery.

On the top landing a tall, stooped figure stood glaring at the commotion like a prison guard watching over inmates during an exercise break at the state pen. Mr. Holmes. Looking up into his red-rimmed eyes, I saw his lips soften into a slight smile at Mama; but when he caught sight of me, they tightened again with disapproval. In seconds, we had swept by his post, but he looked at me with such intensity that I felt like I had received a warning. Against what, I had no idea, but I had a feeling I should keep my hands in plain sight when the collection plate passed through them.

Mama insisted that I sit up toward the front with her, and though I didn't want to look that conspicuous, I did as she asked. I was aware that my purple head was being stared at by every person in the many rows behind me, but only for a little while. As we sang the first hymn, my mind focused on the words and the music, and from then on I was in the house of the Lord, worshiping right along with the rest of them, and I knew He didn't care if my hair was purple or orange or green. He was just glad I was there, and I was glad to be there.

"Mayla, I need a favor. Please say yes. Pleeeeeease!"

Stuart stood in the breezeway outside my apartment door at 6:20 in the morning, a plastic grocery sack in his hand. He wore a gray raincoat over his jeans and tee shirt, but the rain dripped onto his bare head and wet the wooden slat floor all around him. I had gone straight to the shower when I got out of bed, and hadn't bothered to look out my window. It was pouring. Another lovely day in Kentucky.

"Come on in out of the rain, you lunkhead," I said, backing up to allow him to step into the apartment. "What's in the bag?"

He opened it and let me peek inside. "A book. That's the favor. A friend's in the hospital, and I promised I would bring him something to read today, but I forgot I also told Michael I'd run an errand for him on my lunch break, and I won't have time to do both. Could you run it over to him on your lunch?"

He held the sack toward me, his eyes begging. I took another step back.

"I hate hospitals," I informed Stuart. "Take it on your way to work."

"Silly," he said, punching my arm, "visiting hours don't start until later. They don't want people tramping through the hospital at six-thirty a.m."

"So leave it at the front desk."

Stuart heaved a loud sigh. "The whole point of visiting a friend in the hospital is to *visit* him. Alex is gay, and his family hasn't spoken to him since he came out ten years ago. He keeps pretty much to himself, so he doesn't have many friends. He's desperate for company."

I shook my head. "I don't know him. I'm sure he doesn't want some stranger visiting him any more than I want to go."

"C'mon, Mayla. I thought Christians are supposed to visit the sick and all that."

I gave him a sideways look. "Where did you learn that?"

"Hey," he said, looking injured, "I went to Sunday school as a kid. I'm not completely ignorant of these things."

I bit my lip. Stuart was right, of course. I had read in the Bible about visiting the sick and praying for them. I hadn't thought I would be called upon to do it quite so soon, though. Sighing, I took the sack from Stuart.

"Oh, all right," I grumped. "What's his name, and where is he?"

"Alex Markham, in room 347 at Saint Patrick's, and he's not a complete stranger. You've met him before. He and his friend Stephen came to a party with Michael and me once. Thanks Mayla, you're a treasure."

Pleased with his success, Stuart blew a kiss my way as he bounded out into the rain. I closed the door behind him a little harder than necessary. I *hated* hospitals.

"Hey Lord," I prayed as I walked down the hallway to my bedroom to finish getting dressed for work, "I'll do this because the Bible says I should. I just don't feel comfortable about praying with this guy, okay? I wouldn't know what to say, and he probably doesn't want me to anyway. You wouldn't want us both to feel stupid, would you?"

The Lord remained silent, but I didn't feel good about what His answer might be.

The hospital smelled just like I thought it would. Vivid memories of my trips to the hospital where Daddy died crowded into my mind. I suppose lots of people have bad feelings about hospitals for the same reason, but that didn't make me feel any better about going into one. I remembered the time, twelve years earlier, when I had been at the hospital every day for what seemed like months. It had really only been two weeks before Daddy gave in to the injuries caused by his car accident, but every minute of those two weeks had lasted a lifetime. The pungent smell of antiseptic conjured up those days in my mind like they were yesterday. When I caught a glimpse of myself in the shiny metal elevator doors, I was almost surprised to see an adult; for a moment I was ten years old again and holding back the tears that Mama had begged me not to shed in Daddy's room.

I rode up to the third floor and stepped cautiously out into a carpeted corridor. The antiseptic smell was stronger here and mixed with the odors of food wafting from a cart of lunch trays standing by one of the doors to my right. My stomach gave a lurch, and I opened my mouth so I could breathe without smelling the nauseating combination. The sign on the wall indicated that room 347 was to my left, past the nurses' station. I walked that way with a steady step, ignoring the disapproving looks I collected along the way.

The door stood open. The light inside the room was much dimmer than the brightly florescent-lighted corridor, and I wondered why hospital rooms had to look so gloomy. I took a deep breath and said in a low voice, "Okay, Lord, here goes nothing," before stepping through the doorway.

The room held two beds, and the first was empty. A partially closed curtain between the beds gave the occupant on the other side a little privacy from curious eyes in the hallway. Stepping through the doorway, I paused. What if he was using a bedpan or something like that? I cleared my throat to make some noise and said, "Hello?"

"Yes?" Alex's voice was a high tenor, and he sounded tired. "Is that a nurse?"

I stepped around the curtain.

He was propped up in bed on several pillows. I stood very still a moment, staring at him in shock. He was thinner than any human being I had ever seen, so thin that his bald scalp looked like a skeleton with white tissue paper stretched over it. His collarbones protruded sharply beneath the blue-dotted hospital gown, and the skin on his neck was almost the same shade as the white blanket that lay neatly over him without a wrinkle anywhere. His body barely made a lump beneath it. His right arm lay stationary on the mattress alongside him, a tube sticking into the skin just above his wrist, the point of insertion to his skin covered in plastic tape. Vivid, ugly bruises stood out all around that wrist. His arm bones jutted out clearly beneath the paper-white skin, and angry sores dotted both arms. Several brownish spots were prominent on his forehead. Though I had never seen the symptoms in person, I recognized them instantly.

Alex Markham had AIDS.

Either he didn't notice my shock or he chose to ignore it.

"You're Mayla, right? We've met before, about a year ago, though you might not remember me. My hair was darker then."

He laughed and made a feeble gesture with his right hand toward his bald scalp. I laughed with him, but mine sounded hollow, forced. I struggled with the tidal wave of emotions flooding through me, foremost among them a white-hot fury at Stuart for not warning me. I swallowed several times against a suddenly dry throat, and then bravely stuck out my hand.

"Well, it's nice to meet you again, Alex."

He gave a sympathetic smile, but didn't take my hand. He shook his arm just a little, rattling the tube running out of it, and shrugged. Then he nodded toward the lone visitor's chair near the foot of the bed.

"Why don't you pull that over here closer to the bed."

I did as directed, then sat down and looked at him, clutching the sack in my hands. My gaze was drawn, unbidden, to the sores on his head, the dry, cracked lips. I tried to look away, but to where? There was nowhere to look where his disease wasn't evident. My gaze traveled to his eyes, which locked with mine, and I quickly looked down at my hands. I didn't want him to see my horror, which must surely be obvious.

"So, is that the book Stuart sent?"

"Uh, yeah."

I handed him the sack and he pulled out the book. I couldn't even read the title, I was so preoccupied with not looking at Alex or anything to do with him. I examined the equipment around his bed, evil-looking machines and a thing that looked like a plastic blender container with nasty stuff inside it. Just then Alex started to cough—deep, wracking spasms that left him breathless—and he turned his head away from me to spit into a tissue. My stomach flip-flopped, and I had a sudden and frantic desire to cover my mouth with a face mask. Could I catch what he had? I knew I couldn't catch AIDS from a germ in the air, but I also knew that AIDS killed with secondary infections like pneumonia, and I wasn't sure if something like that could be contagious.

"Sorry about that," Alex wheezed, struggling to get his breath. "The coughing is better today, believe it or not."

"Pneumonia?" I asked, trying to calm myself down enough to show some sympathy. That was why I was there, wasn't it?

He nodded. "And KS."

I must have looked blank.

"Kaposi's sarcoma. It's a cancer-like disease common among people with AIDS. It used to be considered harmless, but if you have no immune system to fight it—"

He shrugged, and I nodded.

"They tried to treat it with radiation, but that depletes the immune system even further. That's when the pneumonia set in. My doctor says this could be it, the combination of infections that will finally do me in."

He said it matter-of-factly, like it was no big deal. I felt tears prickle behind my eyeballs, and firmly willed myself not to let them come forward. I looked down at my hands and swallowed again.

"Hey," Alex said in a soft voice that told me he knew I was struggling, "thanks for bringing the book by for Stuart. You've probably got to get back to work or something, so don't feel like you have to stick around."

That was too much. The tears came welling to the front of my eyes and I looked up at him, unable to stop them from slipping down my cheeks.

"I'm sorry, Alex. I'm such a big clunk. I've just never known anyone before who was going to . . . well, you know . . . except my father, and that was a long time ago. In fact, I haven't been in a hospital since he died, and I swore I never would again."

"It must be tough for you, then, coming here to visit me."

I looked at him for a moment, dumbfounded by his concern for me. Suddenly, I found myself laughing. I do that sometimes, laugh at inappropriate times. But the situation was just so ridiculous. I should be concerned for him, and yet all the sympathy and concern in that room was coming from Alex. After all, I was the healthy one who had just found a brand-new life in Jesus. Alex was a gay man lying in a hospital bed alone with no one but a stranger to visit him.

"I'm sorry, Alex," I told him again, "I'm not laughing at you. I'm laughing at myself. I'm such an idiot sometimes."

"I don't think you're an idiot. I think you're brave for coming here at all. Not many people would have."

I hung my head. "I might not have either, if Stuart had told me why you're in here."

Alex made a move as if to sit straight up in the bed. "Stuart didn't tell you? That bum!"

I laughed again. "Yeah, I was thinking a lot worse than 'bum' a minute ago. But he probably knew I would refuse, and he was determined that I come up here today."

Alex settled back more deeply into the pillows.

"I know why he wanted you here. He told me you're a Christian, and he figured since I'm dying anyway it might be about time for me to get a little religion for myself."

I sat abruptly back against the hard plastic of my chair, speechless. There I was telling the Lord I was too embarrassed to pray with a complete stranger, when all the time Stuart, who wasn't even a Christian, had sent me here to tell this guy about Jesus. I was more than a little embarrassed; I was humiliated before God.

"I've got to tell you, Alex, I don't know much about it. I'm a brand-new Christian myself, and I probably can't answer any of your questions. I could have my pastor come by for a visit if you like."

Alex shook his head. "I've seen enough preachers to last a lifetime, especially a short lifetime like mine. I'm not really interested to be honest, but Stuart's a friend, and he told me you would be entertaining if nothing else. So I figured, what the heck? I mean, I've got nothing else on my agenda for the day."

Well, Lord, I thought, *this is a tough place You've put me in. What am I supposed to say to convince this guy that he needs You?*

No sooner than that question popped into my mind, I realized something. Jesus loved Alex. He loved him more than I could ever imagine. He loved him even if he had AIDS and even if he was gay and even if Alex died hating Him. I was suddenly filled with a peace that I knew could only come from God. I knew that my job was not to bring Alex to the Lord. It was the Lord's job to draw him to the cross, just like He had drawn me. My job was to tell Alex a story. And that's all.

"Entertaining, huh?" I grinned with sudden relief. "How about I tell you how I became a Christian in my mama's little church in hot pink 'hooker' panties?"

Alex grinned back at me. "That does sound entertaining."

I spent the next fifteen minutes describing for Alex what had happened to me a little over a week before, and I must have told it well because I had him laughing so hard he had a coughing fit that turned his face purple and made me feel guilty for setting him off. He waved away my apologies, and when he could talk again he thanked me.

"I've got to get back to work." I stood and scooted the chair back where it had been when I came in. "But I've enjoyed meeting you again, Alex. I hope you like the book."

"If you have time, please come back sometime, Mayla," he said, looking a little wistful.

"I look forward to it," I told him.

As I pressed the elevator button, I was amazed to realize that I meant it.

Chapter 5

Sometimes I wonder what the good Lord was thinking when He made women. Oh, all the feminists can just jump down off their soapboxes right now, because I didn't mean that the way it sounded. After all, I'm a woman, too. I certainly don't think the whole female gender is a blight on the species, so don't take it that way.

What I mean is this: I've been dumped by guys, and that hurts. But it hurts a lot more to get dumped by a female friend. I have a theory about that. It's because women make friends easily. We meet, we have lunch, and by the end of the meal we're sharing our deepest, darkest secrets with each other. It takes years to get a guy to tell you his personal secrets, but women tell them to each other within hours of their first hello.

So naturally, when one of those relationships goes sour, we feel personally rejected. We've opened our souls, and it hurts at a deep level to be rejected by someone who knows your innermost secrets.

That's how I felt with Sylvia. I thought she knew and loved and accepted me, the real me. So when I discovered the joy of being a Christian, I thought she would be happy for me. I never expected her to react so badly, and when she did, I saw it as a rejection. At first it hurt, but after a while I got angry.

We didn't see each other much at home because of our work schedules, but we did have to talk quite a bit at The Max. Every time I got an order for an alcoholic drink I had to go to the server's window at the bar and ask Sylvia to get it for me. And she just couldn't do it without making some comment or other about my newfound Christianity.

She'd say, "So what did you learn in church the other day, how to look self-righteous while you're sneering at sinners?"

Or, "Any converts this week, or have you decided to make friends instead of enemies?"

Or even, "What's the news from God lately, Mayla? Any new earthquakes planned, or maybe a tornado?"

For a while, I tried to reason with her, but she was so nasty that I learned pretty quickly to ignore her. Her rejection hurt, and all the more because I didn't understand why she was so bitterly angry with me. Had I misjudged our relationship? Maybe we had never really been friends at all.

"A gin and tonic and a glass of white zin," I'd say, not giving her the satisfaction of a sarcastic reply.

Jolene posted the work schedules on Saturday mornings, and the second Saturday after I became a Christian I reported to work and checked the following week's roster. I rechecked it and then called Jolene at home.

"There's a problem," I said. "I told you I can't work Sundays until four, but you've scheduled me tomorrow at eleven."

Jolene, obviously just awakened, answered, "Sylvia told me yesterday that you could work tomorrow. She's your roommate so I thought she would know. I hope that's okay, because I couldn't find anyone else to work that shift."

Hearing anxiety in her voice, I sighed. "I guess it's okay this time. From now on, I don't work on Sundays until four, no matter what *anyone* says, okay?"

"Sure Mayla. And thanks for covering tomorrow."

I hung up the phone and marched over to the bar.

"Who do you think you are," I demanded of Sylvia. "You do not set my schedule. You never have, so what gives you the right now?"

She gave me a sickly sweet smile and kept on drying glasses and hanging them on the rack above her head.

"It's for your own good, Mayla. If you're working, you can't be running off to that poisonous little church and having your mind filled with that garbage. That stuff isn't for us, no matter what you think right now. You just need to get away from it for a while, and you'll see I'm right."

She was so condescending, so *self-righteous,* that I wanted to scream. I took a deep breath and bit back all the words that itched to get out of my mouth. How dare she try to manipulate me? How dare she try to keep me away from my church?

"In the future," I said evenly through gritted teeth, "I'll thank you not to interfere with my schedule. I am old enough to determine for myself what is right for me and what isn't. I don't need you to manage my life, and your interference is not welcome."

Sylvia's lips tightened into a thin line. "Fine. I was only trying to save you from them. From now on I won't bother."

I turned and walked away, trying to control my anger.

Lord, I prayed, *what is her problem?*

Why is it that everyone assumes all young women are good with children? It's as if there's an unspoken belief that every unmarried female aches to have kids and will therefore gladly spend all her free time playing with the babies in the church nursery. Or maybe it's a misconception that all women have a God-given talent that enables them to teach kids and like it.

Salliesburg Independent Christian Church will not make that mistake again.

Pastor Paul had said to me after church one Sunday, "Mayla, we need to find you a place to serve."

"I already serve," I told him. "I do it at night. The pay's not great, but the tips are better than some other places I could name."

"That's not what I meant," he chuckled. "I'm talking about serving Christ by getting involved in His church. It's part of how you grow in your Christian walk, by doing something for Him. Some people teach Sunday school, some sing in the choir, some prepare the communion each Sunday, that sort of thing."

Just then, he got called away and we didn't get to finish our conversation. I thought about it, though, and decided he was right. But I didn't have a clue where to start looking to get involved in serving at the church. So, a few Sundays later, when I walked through the door and was accosted by Mrs. McAnley, I had been primed.

"Mayla," she said, grabbing my arm and therefore effectively cutting off my only means of escape, "I need your help.

Julie Longwood is sick this morning, and I need someone to do children's church."

"Do children's church?"

"It's no big deal, really, you just lead them in a few songs, tell a story from the Bible, ask them if they have any prayer requests, that sort of thing. Mostly you keep them quiet so they don't disturb the worship service."

That didn't sound too hard. Mama had a look of mild alarm on her face, which should have told both me and Mrs. McAnley something.

"I don't think Mayla—"

"Nonsense." Mrs. McAnley pulled me forcefully toward the stairs, dismissing Mama's objections unheard. "Mayla will do just fine. Let me show you where things are before Sunday school."

There didn't seem to be much use resisting, so I followed blindly along. Like a sheep to the slaughter, as the saying goes. Mrs. McAnley was flatteringly appreciative that I agreed to do it, fawning all over me as she showed me the Fellowship Hall full of little chairs all lined up in rows with a big one in the front. She even showed me a book of children's Bible stories I could read from if I wanted to.

"But if you have a story from the Bible yourself, the children would love to hear it."

We walked into the little kitchen, and she pointed out the big pitcher of Kool-Aid and a couple of bags of cookies to give them for a snack after the Bible story.

"Okay," I said, "and then what? Do they play games or something?"

"As long as they're quiet," she warned with a stern look. "The sanctuary is right above you and sound carries, so keep them quiet."

I got the last of my instructions in a rush before Mrs. McAnley gave me a hug of thanks and slipped into her Sunday school class. I turned to head toward mine and nearly ran right into a tall, thin figure standing silently in the middle of the hallway. Mr. Holmes. He glowered down at me as he always did, as if I were a cockroach that had found its way into his kitchen and was about to become acquainted with the bottom of his boot.

"Excuse me," I murmured, stepping around him and trying to ignore the daggers being thrown at me from beneath his spiky gray eyebrows.

Then I stopped. Though I had grown accustomed to people staring, I didn't often find myself on the receiving end of a glare like Mr. Holmes's. It rubbed me the wrong way, and especially in church, where in my opinion people ought to smile more often than they frown.

I turned back to him and looked up into his watery blue eyes. "You don't like me much, do you Mr. Holmes?"

The scraggly eyebrows shot up. He hadn't expected me to call him on his behavior, I suspected. I kept my eyes locked on his, demanding an answer. After a moment, he gave a snort.

"Got no reason to like ye," he said, his gaze dropping for a second to my labret stud.

I felt my back stiffen. "You've got no reason to dislike me either, but for some reason you do."

He shrugged. "Don't particularly like ye, but I don't hate yer guts neither."

He started to move away, but I wasn't going to let him off that easily. "Then why do you stare at me all the time?"

He laughed, a quick and sarcastic blast. "Young 'uns who do themselves up like 'at are askin' to be stared at, ain't they?"

"Not the way you stare," I shot back. "You act like you

think I'm going to whip out a gun and demand people's jewelry. You make me feel like I'm not good enough to be a part of this church."

His eyelids narrowed. "Church's fer everbody, I know that. But ye cain't 'spect ever'body to like ye right off. Ye ain't done nuthin' to prove yersel' good or bad yet."

Taking a deep breath to steady my rising temper, I spoke deliberately. "So I have to prove myself? Is that how it works for everyone, or just for people who look like me?"

His gaze swept up to my hair and then to my nose and lip studs before returning to my eyes. "Everbody's gotta prove sumpthin'. Some jest makes it harder on theirselves than others."

With that he walked away, leaving me alone in the hallway, fuming. I had to prove myself, did I? Well, I would, and I'd do it today. I'd be the best children's church teacher Salliesburg Independent Christian Church had ever seen, and that would show Mr. Holmes just who he was dealing with.

I slipped into my Sunday school class, which had already begun. I had a hard time concentrating on Sam's lesson because I was planning my own. I had been studying the Bible regularly, and I figured I could come up with a pretty decent lesson that a kid could understand. Besides making a point to Mr. Holmes, it would give me a chance to talk to someone other than Pastor Paul about the stuff I was leaning. I certainly had no audience in Sylvia.

By the time Sam led us in prayer and dismissed us, I was looking forward to children's church. It was a place to serve, as Pastor Paul had said. It was a chance to show off my newfound knowledge. The kids would love me. They would go home and tell their parents how great children's church had been, how much they had learned, how cool their new teacher was.

Mama grabbed my elbow as I left the room.

"I'm gonna help you with children's church," she announced with a look that brooked no argument. Which of course immediately made me want to argue.

"No way," I said, pulling my elbow out of her grasp. "I can handle it myself."

"Mayla," she said in a whisper, looking around to be sure she wasn't overheard, "you don't like kids. Remember Rebecca Barnes."

Rebecca Barnes was the one and only kid I ever babysat as a teenager. Her parents believed spanking was corporal punishment and that a four-year-old should be reasoned with and then allowed to make her own decisions. Rebecca's decision was to lure me into the basement with cries of monsters down there, and then lock the door behind me while she proceeded to eat an entire half-gallon of chocolate ice cream on the living room sofa. When the parents came home a couple hours later, they found a sticky chocolate mess, a sick kid, and a fuming teenager pounding on the basement door demanding to be let out. When that door opened, I came storming out ready to see retribution done on that child's backside. What I got instead was, "Rebecca, do you see that what you did was wrong? Aren't you sorry? See, Mayla, she's sorry."

I don't know what happened to Rebecca Barnes, but I'll bet she holds a position of authority in a juvenile detention center somewhere.

"This is different," I told Mama. "First of all, I'm older now and I'm not about to be tricked like that again. Second, these are church kids. And third, there's no basement."

Mama would have argued further, but just then Alice Engelmann came by and drafted her to help stuff a last minute announcement into the bulletins. I wandered upstairs to speak with Pastor Paul before the service.

When the organist began the prelude, the last few people filed quickly into the sanctuary to take their seats, and I went to the bathroom. I don't mind admitting that I went in there more to spend a few nervous minutes alone than to use the facilities. When I came out, stomach fluttering, the hallway had emptied. The sanctuary doors had been closed, and I could hear the drone of Brother Damon's voice making the morning announcements. I went down the deserted stairs to the Fellowship Hall, pausing at the bottom for a fortifying breath before I opened the door.

At first glance, there appeared to be at least four hundred children engaged in a variety of actions that would certainly have earned them spankings at home, and jail time elsewhere. In the corner, a couple of older boys held a skinny kid upside down by the feet while they emptied his pockets, and a group of little girls nearby intently colored on the wall. A kid sat up in the serving window that led into the kitchen, pouring communion juice from a plastic jug into the open mouths of a pair of purple-faced boys on the floor. A group of little ones raced from one wall to the other, shrieking their glee, and three older girls sat Indian-style in the middle of a table in the center of the room, brushing each others' hair, oblivious to the chaos around them.

Completely at a loss, I felt my lower jaw drop. I stood there for a moment, ignored, before I realized that someone needed to take charge. I guessed that someone was me. I stepped forward and attempted to get their attention.

"Excuse me, please."

They continued to ignore me. I doubt if they even noticed I was there. I judged more volume was needed, so I shouted louder.

"Uh, hey, everybody, could you be quiet and listen for a minute?"

Nothing. I decided that being polite wasn't going to work, so I took a deep breath and bellowed, "All right you little monsters, shut up and sit down!"

That did the trick. All sound ceased as they turned to look at me in shock. Maybe it was my imagination, but it seemed that even upstairs there was a pause in the organ music. One of the primping girls on the table gave a little gasp when she caught sight of me, like she had come face-to-face with a vampire.

"What did you call us?" One of the bigger boys who had been shaking down the skinny kid glared at me through narrow eyelids.

"I called you monsters," I replied, "because that's what you're acting like. You're in a church, for cryin' out loud, and you're acting like street hoodlums. Now whatever you took from that kid, give it back right now."

"We didn't take anything," his buddy said.

"Yes you did," the skinny kid argued hotly. "You took my dollar I got last night for my tooth."

I walked over to the trio and stuck my hand, palm up, into the face of the biggest of the two bullies.

"Hand it over."

He stared me down for a minute, but I can look pretty tough when I want to. In no time at all his gaze dropped, and he grudgingly put the dollar into my hand. I handed it to the skinny kid, who shoved it into his pocket and ran across the room, out of reach. I gave the two tough guys another good glare, then turned to the boy on the counter.

"You there, get something to clean up that mess," I said, pointing to the purple juice all over the floor. "And you two down there on the floor, go wash your faces and get back here."

The rest of them were staring at me, still frozen where they were. I glared around the room, determined to show them that I was in charge, and I wasn't going to take any guff. One of the girls on the table giggled nervously and was quickly shushed by her friends.

"All right," I told them, "my name is Mayla Strong, and Mrs. McAnley asked me to handle children's church today. So let's get started. I want everyone over here by this wall. Line up."

Nobody moved.

"Come on," I said louder, "move it!"

They moved it. I did a head count and discovered that what I had at first taken for four hundred kids was really only fourteen. The bullies were the oldest, and the rest of them ranged in age and size all the way down to one little girl who looked like she was barely out of diapers. That little girl did not join the others against the wall, but stood directly in front of me, her head tilted back as far as it would go, staring up at me with wide blue eyes and a wet, gaping mouth.

I looked down at her. A cute little thing, she wore one of those frilly pink dresses with white tights and shiny black shoes. But the way she stared at me made me nervous.

"Who is this?" I asked the room at large.

A boy with blonde hair came hastily forward, grabbed the girl by the hand and pulled her back in line with him, mumbling, "She's my sister. C'mon Jessica."

I let my glare sweep them all once more, then asked in a much calmer voice, "What are you supposed to be doing right now?"

One or two hesitant hands went up, and I pointed to a girl with curly brown hair.

"We're supposed to be sitting in those chairs over there?" Her voice rose at the end as if asking a question.

"Right," I said, glaring. "So get there."

They almost ran across the room to the rows of chairs.

I waited until everyone had taken a seat before I sat down in the single adult chair at the front of the room. It felt a little strange, I'll admit, having twenty-eight eyes staring at me, waiting for me to tell them what to do. I cast about frantically in my mind for a moment. What was supposed to come next? Oh, yes! Music!

"You," I said, pointing toward a buzz-headed kid in the front, "what's your favorite song?"

The kid looked like he had just been singled out for a go in the electric chair. His mouth opened as he tried to answer, but no sound came out. The oldest of the bullies snickered, and I rounded on him.

"What's your name, kid?"

He stared at me insolently a moment before answering. "Brandon."

"You think singing is funny, Brandon?" I asked, daring him to say yes.

"Depends on who's doing it," he responded with a smirk toward his buddy.

I had to admit it was a good answer, but I didn't let on. "How about you doing it?"

The smirk disappeared. "Huh?"

"I said, how about if you sing a song for us."

All movement stopped as everyone waited to see how he would answer me. He glanced around the room, gathering courage from the others before he looked back up at me. The smirk returned and he said, "I don't want to, and you can't make me."

I have never responded well when someone challenges me, and this was obviously a direct challenge to my authority.

"I can make you." Though quiet, my voice was full of steel.

"No you can't," he said again, louder this time. "You can't make me do nothing. You ain't my mother. You ain't even the regular church lady. You're just a substitute. Substitutes can't make you do stuff, and I ain't gonna sing."

The watching kids drew an audible intake of breath. Several of their mouths dropped open in amazement at Brandon's nerve, impressed with his courage. I knew I had to put the little brat in his place before I lost all control of the situation.

Bending over until my face was inches away from his, I whispered in a voice overheard by almost everyone in the otherwise silent room.

"I have friends who could make you disappear without a trace. Do you believe that?"

Brandon's eyes grew round as he stared into mine. His gaze dropped briefly to take in first the ruby-colored stone in my nostril and then the cross below my lip, then snapped back up to my eyes as he nodded.

"Then don't mess with me, kid."

In retrospect, this was probably not the most diplomatic way to handle the situation. But at least Brandon remained completely silent through the rest of children's church.

I couldn't get a volunteer to sing, and since I didn't know even one kid's song, I decided to skip the music and get right to the Bible lesson. I have to say I enjoyed that part. I told a story I had read in the book of Acts that I thought had a good lesson, especially for Brandon and his criminal friend. It was about Ananias and Sapphira, who decided to cheat the Lord out of some money. The kids stayed very quiet through the whole story, their attention completely fixed on me as I paced back and forth in front of them, gesturing with my hands the

way Pastor Paul did when he preached. At the end, when first
Ananias and then Sapphira got struck down dead right there
in front of the whole church, one of the girls started to cry.

"What's wrong with you?" I asked, rounding on her.

She didn't answer, just sobbed silently.

"You don't steal, do you?"

She shook her head.

"Then you don't have anything to worry about."

After that, I had them file one by one into the kitchen
area to get a cup of Kool-Aid and a couple of cookies. They
returned to their seats to eat, no one saying a word. In the
kitchen I put the Kool-Aid pitcher in the refrigerator, silently
congratulating myself on a fine job of keeping them quiet. It
would take them a few minutes to eat, and then I'd let them
talk quietly among themselves for a while before their parents
came to get them.

Then I caught sight of the clock on the wall, and felt like I
had been punched in the stomach. It had been fifteen minutes.
I still had forty-five minutes to go.

Promising myself that I would never volunteer for children's church again, I went resolutely back into the Fellowship
Hall and took my seat in the front of the room.

"Well," I asked the sea of subdued faces, "what do you want
to do next?"

Silence.

"Come on, doesn't anyone have any ideas? Any games we
can play? Quiet games," I added sternly.

Nothing.

"How about questions? Does anyone have any questions
about the Bible lesson?"

Tentatively, one of the primping girls on the back row
raised a hand.

"How long have you had your nose pierced?"

Not exactly the sort of question I had in mind, but if it killed time . . .

"Almost two years," I told her.

"Did it hurt?"

I shrugged. "Worse than my ear, but not as bad as my lip."

One of her friends raised a hand and asked, "What happens if you have a runny nose? Does it get all gross?"

Someone giggled, and I sighed. You would be surprised how often that question came up.

"It hasn't happened so far," I told her.

The questions kept coming as they gained courage. They wanted to know if I had anything else pierced, and then they wanted to know where I worked and if I had a boyfriend. Everyone listened, the boys kept quiet, and before I knew it I heard the sound of the organ playing the final hymn above us. I had survived an entire hour of children's church.

At the sight of the first parent coming through the door, chaos returned and the kids scattered. Having served my time, I left as well and went to find Mama upstairs.

"How did it go?" she asked, her expression anxious.

"Great," I told her. "No problem."

Pastor Paul called me the following Tuesday night.

"Mayla, I've had a few calls from some concerned parents," he said without preamble.

"Yeah? Concerned about what?"

"Well, it seems that some of the children were a little frightened by your lesson at children's church on Sunday."

"Frightened?" I asked, surprised. "But it was from the Bible."

"Yes, but they apparently feel that Ananias and Sapphira isn't an appropriate lesson for some of the younger children."

I considered that for a moment. "Maybe they're right, but a couple of the older ones sure did need to hear it." I told him about catching Brandon and his buddy stealing the skinny kid's money. He listened and then asked, "Would that be the boy you threatened to make disappear if he didn't sing in front of the group?"

His voice sounded the tiniest bit annoyed. I shifted the phone uneasily to the other ear. "Well, yeah, but it wasn't exactly like that."

"I see." He coughed uncomfortably. "Did you enjoy teaching children's church?"

"Not exactly. I really didn't want to do it, but Mrs. McAnley was in a rough spot, and I thought it was a good place to serve, like you said." I paused before confessing, "I'm not really a kid person."

"So you don't want to do it again, then?"

"Definitely not," I told him.

"That's good." He sounded relieved. "We'll keep looking for a place you can serve, Mayla. I'm sure we can come up with something more suitable for you."

I felt a wave of relief too. "Okay, Pastor Paul."

Chapter 6

When Alex was released from the hospital, I didn't see him for a while, though I did call a few times to check on him. His roommate, Stephen, was not a friendly guy.

Then, as is typical with people suffering from AIDS, Alex caught another infection and had to be readmitted to Saint Patrick's. I started dropping by the hospital on my lunch hours for quick visits. Alex was always so glad to see me, and I enjoyed our talks. A friendship developed between us. I told him about my problems with Sylvia, and he was a great listener. He didn't open up to me much, but instead seemed content to get me started on a subject and then listen as I rambled. I knew he looked forward to my visits to break the monotony of his long hospital days, so I went as often as I could.

When I got off the elevator one Sunday evening and turned toward Alex's room, a nurse approached me. She was one of the younger ones, probably only a few years older than me, a blonde with wide-set brown eyes and skin that still showed traces of teenage acne. The hospital badge pinned to the front of her scrubs told me her name: Gail.

"Excuse me, you're Alex Markham's friend, aren't you?"

"That's right."

"I've seen you here a lot, so I thought it might be a good idea to talk to you about something. You know why he's in the hospital?"

She had a very direct stare, one that made me want to squirm, and a no-nonsense manner that gave her an air of authority contrary to her youth. She wasn't your typical Florence Nightingale-type nurse.

"I know he has AIDS, yes."

"Do you know how serious it is?"

I cocked my head to one side. "Why don't you tell me?"

She glanced around the hallway. "I shouldn't say this, since you're not a family member, but to be honest, he's dying. And it isn't going to be long, either."

Alex told me the first time I met him that he expected to die soon, and recently I had seen it in his face. Still, I couldn't help the tears that filled my eyes when I heard the official words. Nurse Gail ignored them and went on.

"I looked in his file, and he didn't list any next of kin. The only emergency contact he has is his friend Mr. Walker." Her face became carefully impassive. "Frankly, he hasn't been here much, and when he is he avoids talking to me or to any of the other nurses. I have been trying to get Alex to tell me if he has any family we can call, but he says he's an orphan, and there isn't anyone."

"An orphan, huh?" I shook my head. I thought I remembered Stuart saying Alex's parents didn't speak to him, but not that they were dead.

"I don't believe him," she said, "but I can't get anything else out of him. So I thought maybe you could talk to him, see what you can find out."

I hesitated. "If he says there isn't anyone to call, maybe you should just leave it alone. If he does have family, maybe there's a reason he doesn't want them here."

She looked squarely into my eyes. "If he does have family, I think we both know why they're not here. I don't care about that. Alex is dying. No one should die alone."

That stopped me. She was right.

"I'll see what I can do," I promised.

Maybe I saw with fresh eyes after my conversation with the nurse, but Alex looked worse than ever. It didn't seem possible for him to be frailer than he had been just two days before, but I swear he was. Even talking exhausted him.

"Hey, Mayla. Glad you stopped by." The effort to greet me robbed him of breath. He drew in a deep one. "How was church this week? Any new disasters to report?"

Alex seemed really interested in my "church escapades," as he called them. He had gotten a big kick out of the Bible story I told the kids that had them in tears, and he often had me describe Pastor Paul's sermons to him. So far he had steadfastly refused the offer of a visit from the preacher so he could hear one direct from the horse's mouth, so to speak. Instead he liked to hear me repeat it in my own words, which he said were much more entertaining than any preacher could be.

"No new disasters," I told him. "I'm trying to keep a low profile these days. How you doing?"

"Oh, about the same. Stuart stopped by last night, and it was good to see him."

"Has anyone else been here?"

"No."

I had suspected that Stephen Walker, Alex's partner, had been coming less and less frequently. The nurse had just confirmed it. I knew Alex must really be hurting, but he had never discussed it with me and I didn't push.

"Uh, listen, Alex. You've never mentioned your family. Do they live around here?"

Rolling his eyes, he said, "Nurse Gail has been talking to you, hasn't she?"

"Well, yeah. She said—"

"I don't care what she said. She's a busybody and needs to keep her nose in her own business."

I looked him in the eye. "Maybe she's right, Alex. I mean, do your parents even know you're sick?" He turned his head toward the window and didn't answer. "Maybe you need to at least tell them that much. They probably would want to know."

When he turned back to me I saw a terrible sadness in his eyes. "It wouldn't matter to them, Mayla. Trust me."

"But—"

"Can we not talk about this anymore?"

Pushing him any further was useless, at least for the moment. But I wasn't going to give up.

"Okay," I told him. "How about if I tell you instead about today's sermon? It was a good one."

He smiled and settled deeper back into his pillow. "Tell me about it."

When I left, Nurse Gail sat at the nurse's station, scribbling on a chart. She looked up at me, her eyebrows arched like question marks, and I just shook my head as I walked by.

I pounded on Stuart's door that night. It was almost eleven, but I knew he'd be up. He answered the door in a maroon silk bathrobe.

"Funny time for a social call, Mayla," he told me with a scowl.

"Yeah, I know, but this is important. It's about Alex."

He clutched the door. "Oh no, he didn't—"

I shook my head. "Not yet, but that's what I need to talk to you about."

"Come on in here."

I stepped through the doorway and into his apartment, which was the same layout as mine and Sylvia's, only you wouldn't recognize it unless you looked hard. I always felt like I was in Africa when I visited Stuart and Michael. They had a red leather sofa and chair with dozens of animal-stripe pillows. The coffee and end tables were thick pieces of glass resting on the backs of four elephants, all atop a large zebra rug. The lamps were made of wood, carved and stained to look like giraffes with painted canvas lampshades, and all over the walls hung up-close pictures of jungle animals. I know it sounds strange, but the effect was—well, yeah, it was strange. I always had a crazy urge to give a loud Tarzan yell and swing from the chandelier above the dinette set.

"Do you know anything about Alex's family?" I asked after I had rearranged a couple of pillows to make a place for myself.

Stuart shrugged. "Only that they haven't spoken to him in years."

"Any idea where they live?"

He cocked his head and gave me a suspicious look. "Why?"

I told him about my conversation with Gail, and then what Alex had said.

"I just can't leave it at that, Stuart. That nurse was right. Nobody should die alone, and apparently he doesn't even have Stephen around much anymore."

"Michael and I have tried to talk to Stephen, but he won't listen to us. He's distant. Between you and me, I don't like him much. I think he has decided to move on, only he doesn't have the guts to tell Alex that. But you're wrong about Alex not having anyone. He has us."

I shook my head. "That's not enough, Stuart. I only met him a few weeks ago, and last time I checked you aren't going to visit him every day any more than I am."

He sighed. "Yeah, I know. And when I do go I can't think of anything to say. Alex and I have never been close, just casual friends really."

"You never heard him say where he's from?"

"I think he said once that he went to high school somewhere in eastern Kentucky. Pikeville, maybe? Yeah, I think that was it."

"Do you think you could call Stephen and see if he knows anything that might help us find his family? A name would be great."

Stuart cocked his head uncertainly. "I'll try, but I doubt if I'll get anything out of him. Maybe I'll ask Michael to try. I think Stephen likes him better than me."

I stood and walked to the door.

"Let me know what you find out," I told him as I let myself out.

"Mayla," Alison said to me the next morning, "you know what I did this weekend?"

We had been getting along better since I stopped talking nasty to people, and I had even started to like her a little. The things that used to irritate me about Alison—her perfect fingernails and tailored jackets with matching shoes—were really the same thing as my facial jewelry; they were her way of making a statement in her world. In a construction company, someone who dresses like Alison stands out as much as someone like me in a fancy department store.

"What?" I asked, slicing into a piece of Monday morning mail.

"I went to church."

I shot her a surprised look. We had not talked about church since the day after I was baptized.

"Why? Couldn't you sleep?"

Her lips twisted wryly at my reference to our last conversation, when she'd told me she liked to sleep in on Sundays. "Actually, I figured if you could manage to get up on Sunday mornings and drive all the way to another town, I could at least try to go half a block."

"So where'd you go?"

She lifted her shoulders a fraction. "There's a Methodist church down the street from my apartment. It's not very big, and the pastor is kind of old, but he preached a good sermon. At least he didn't yell and pound on the pulpit like I remember the preacher doing when I was a kid. The people were real friendly."

"Are you gonna go back?" I asked.

She gave a shy smile. "Yeah, I think I might. There was this one woman who told me she hoped I would come again, and I sort of think she meant it."

One woman at church spoke to a stranger, and it had made enough impression that Alison planned to go back again. That was something I wanted to remember.

"That's great, Alison. I hope it works out for you there."

Then her phone rang and she was summoned to Mr. Clark's office. It was back to business as usual.

I picked up my cell phone and dialed.

"Pastor Paul? It's Mayla Strong."

"Hello, Mayla! How's your week going?"

"Pretty good. I've been thinking about something you said in your sermon last week."

"Oh?" He gave a chuckle. "I'm glad to hear it. Sometimes I think no one out there hears a word I say. It must have been something good for you to remember it for more than a week."

"Well it sure has stuck with me. It was about forgiving people who've hurt you."

"Ah, yes."

"Well," I said slowly, "I've been thinking about it and I have one question. What if I don't forgive them? I mean, even when I know I should because Jesus said to, what if I can't feel forgiveness toward that person. I have tried, but I just can't. Does the Lord hold that against me?"

There was one of Pastor Paul's long pauses, and I knew he was praying for the right words to say. It pleased me that he prayed before he answered my questions. That meant he took me seriously, and that my questions were good ones. It gave me a feeling that maybe I was on the right track. Sort of.

"Have you ever heard of Corrie Ten Boom?" he asked.

The name sounded familiar, but I couldn't place it. "Maybe."

"She survived the Nazi concentration camps in World War II. She wrote a book called *The Hiding Place*."

"I've heard of that," I said.

"At the end of that book she describes a time when she meets a Nazi soldier who had worked in one of the camps she had been in. She had been speaking on forgiveness, and this man was in her audience. When he approached her, she stood looking at him and was overcome by hatred. But she knew the Lord wanted her to forgive him. She had been traveling around preaching about forgiveness since the war ended, but when it came to a personal decision, she couldn't do it."

"What did she do?"

"She prayed. She told the Lord she couldn't do it without His help. She said the hardest thing she ever did was to reach out and shake that Nazi guard's hand. She had to act out her forgiveness even if she didn't feel it. When she did, the Lord allowed her to feel His love for that man. Then it was easy to feel forgiveness for him. True forgiveness isn't something we can do alone, Mayla. It's not something we feel, it's something we do. God has to work His forgiveness in us. Our job is to be obedient and allow Him to do it. Remember when Jesus told the apostles that they should keep forgiving even if someone sinned against them seven times in one day?"

"Yeah." It was in Luke, the first book I had read in the Bible.

"Remember what the apostles said?"

"Uh, no." Well, geesh, I couldn't be expected to remember everything, could I?

"They cried, 'Lord, increase our faith!' They knew they couldn't do what Jesus asked without a strong faith. And neither can we. Does that help?"

"You know," I told him, "it does. I think I know what I'm going to do now. Thanks."

"Any time," he said, and he sounded like he meant it. "See you Sunday?"

"You bet."

Dear Grandmother,

Surprise! It's me, your long-lost granddaughter. Been a long time, huh? I hope you're doing well, and Aunt Louise is okay and all that. Tell her I said hello.

Listen, I'm writing because I wanted to tell you something. I became a Christian last month. Yeah, I know that'll be an even bigger surprise than getting a letter from me, but it's true. And since I was baptized I've been doing a lot of thinking about you. And I've been praying about you, too.

Remember the last time I saw you? You were yelling at Mama and saying if she signed the order for the hospital to unplug that respirator she would rot in hell and you would never speak to her or to me again. Well, we both know what happened. You kept your word, and you haven't spoken to me since. I wanted to tell you that it hurt me a lot. I always thought we had a special relationship, you and me. The first birthday I had after Daddy died was pretty tough, and I really needed you. I know you're far away in Florida, but I missed your phone calls and your letters and visiting in the summer and all.

I have to be honest here and tell you that I didn't cry too much, though. When you didn't call me on my birthday, I cried for a day or so, but then I got mad at you. I have been mad at you ever since, Grandmother, really mad.

When I started writing this letter, I wanted to tell you that I forgive you for deserting me. I've been reading the Bible and going to church and I know it's important to forgive the people who have hurt you. But now I think maybe I need to ask you to forgive me. I could have written to you a long time ago, but I was still too caught up in being angry. I know how hard it was for me to lose my daddy, and for Mama to lose her husband. I just never realized how hard it must have been for you to lose your son. Your only son. I should have been there for you. I'm sorry I wasn't. Please forgive me.

Love,
Mayla

Tears wet my cheeks as I licked the envelope, but I felt good. At peace.

"Lord," I whispered as I dropped the letter into the mailbox, "thank you for teaching me about forgiveness. I hope you can get through to Grandmother, too. Amen."

Chapter 7

A few days after I sent the letter to my grandmother, I came home from work to find Sylvia leafing through a magazine. She was curled up in a corner of the couch with her legs tucked underneath her and only the tips of her bright red toenails peeking out. Her dark hair was pulled back into an untidy knot at the top of her head, and she wore ripped jeans and a tee shirt, which meant that she didn't have any plans for the evening. That was unusual for Sylvia—she usually had a date with a different guy every night of the week.

Now I have to admit something that's a little embarrassing. I had been reading the Bible and learning all the do's and don'ts, and I had started to develop a rather condescending attitude toward Sylvia. Excited about everything I was learning, I had started looking down my nose at her, mostly because she had become so hostile toward me. I didn't consciously try to be mean or hurt her, but my attitude must have been pretty hard to take.

"What, no date tonight?" I asked as I dropped my backpack on the dinette table. That could have been an innocent comment, but I didn't try to filter the righteous disapproval out of my tone. Sylvia flared immediately.

"What's that supposed to mean?" she snapped.

I raised my eyebrows. "What do you think it means?"

"I think it means you disapprove of my dates," she said, "which is something I told you would happen when you first started this religious garbage. I also told you I wouldn't put up with it, so you'd better just drop it right now."

She went back to her magazine, flipping the pages violently.

"I don't disapprove of your dates," I told her. "I disapprove of you letting all those guys spend the night."

"Aha," she said, slamming the magazine closed, "so it's sex you disapprove of. I thought as much. They've corrupted you, just like I said they would."

"I don't disapprove of sex," I told her, "but sex outside of marriage is wrong. Any idiot these days knows how dangerous it is to sleep around. And yes, it does say so in the Bible, which I happen to believe is true."

It really did take some courage for me to make that statement. I mean, I want to be honest here: I had not exactly been an innocent in this area before I met Christ. Sylvia, being my roommate, knew it.

"That is just a little hard to take from you, Mayla. Shall we make a list and compare the guys who have stayed overnight in this apartment?"

I put a sweet but insincere smile on my face. "I'm a new creation in Christ Jesus. Second Corinthians five, verse seventeen. That means my past has been forgiven and I've started new."

"Really? And in your readings have you gotten to the part that says, 'If any one of you is without sin, cast the first stone'? John, chapter eight, verse seven."

That surprised me. Of course I had read that story about the woman caught in adultery and how Jesus saved her from being stoned to death. How in the world did Sylvia know it? Not only know it, know it well enough to be able to quote book, chapter, and verse! I felt myself slipping off my pedestal a bit, and I made a mental note to look it up and check the reference.

"If I remember correctly, Jesus then told that woman to go on her way and stop sinning," I replied, a little less self-righteously.

She smiled, really more of a smirk. "Ah. Of course by 'sinning,' he meant sleeping around. I suppose you buy in to the idea that a woman should have sex with only one man in her whole life."

I started to get a little uncomfortable. Forgiven or not, I realized that I was something of a pot talking to a kettle, but I plowed ahead anyway. "Yeah, I do."

"And the man? Is he supposed to only have one woman for his whole life?"

"Of course."

"Like Adam and Eve," she said.

"That's right."

"Then what about King David?"

That stopped me. "Huh?"

"That Bible of yours calls David a man after God's own heart, and it also says he had more than eight wives."

I couldn't think of a thing to say. I had not read that in the Bible.

Sylvia kept going. "Not only that, but his son Solomon was one of the greatest kings of all times. People came from all over to ask him questions because of his famous wisdom. But that wise king had hundreds of wives and concubines. Probably had sex with a different woman every night of his life."

"He did?"

Sylvia smirked. "Before you start preaching, you had better read that Bible and get all the facts, honey. Start with First Chronicles. And get off my back. I don't want to hear about it."

She opened her magazine and went back to flipping through the pages. I stood there for a minute, stunned, then went to my room. I picked up my cell phone and dialed Pastor Paul's number.

"Hello?"

"It's Mayla." I spoke as quietly as I could.

He answered in a friendly voice, as always. "Hi, Mayla! What's up?"

"I have a question."

He remained quiet while I recounted the conversation I'd just had with Sylvia. He listened without interrupting, and when I finished, he said, "Hmmm."

"Hmmm?" I demanded. "Is that all you have to say?"

"What do you want me to say?"

"I want you to tell me it's not true, that's what I want you to say."

"Sorry, but I can't do that. It is true."

I sucked in a long, deep breath, digesting that. "You mean David had hundreds of wives?"

"Well, I don't know how many wives David had, but the Bible lists some of them by name, and there was definitely more than one. Scripture also says that Solomon had seven hundred wives of royal birth and three hundred concubines."

"Well!" I said, indignant. "That sure doesn't sound like something the apostle Paul would approve of!"

Pastor Paul laughed out loud. "It doesn't, does it? Keep in mind that the Bible does not say God approved of it either. There's a lot of history in the Bible put there for our benefit, but sometimes it's there for us to learn from, not to emulate. As far as David is concerned, the book of Acts does quote God as identifying David as a man after His own heart. It's talking about the time when God called David to replace Saul as king, and at that time David was an unmarried young man, a shepherd, and a skilled musician who spent his time writing and singing praise songs to the Lord. I believe it was the deep love God saw in David's heart that pleased Him so much, and that deep love for God never changed throughout David's life."

"But if he was a man after God's own heart and he had all those wives—" I said.

"Mayla, God seeks a humble heart, a contrite spirit. David had that. He sinned like we all do. He also committed adultery with another man's wife and had the man killed so he could marry her. God hates sin, and He called David on it. The Bible doesn't say David was perfect; none of us is. That doesn't mean God didn't love David. He could see inside David's heart, and what He saw there pleased Him. But if you read about David's entire life, he had lots of problems that resulted from those wives and the kids he had by them."

"And Solomon? Seven *hundred* wives?"

"Ah yes, Solomon. All those wives caused him some major problems with God. Read First Kings, chapter eleven. You'll see. But there's something more interesting about your conversation with Sylvia."

I knew where he was going. "Yeah, I know. How does she know this stuff? I would have sworn she's never picked up a Bible in her life, but she knew this firsthand. She quoted the Bible better than I could."

"Exactly. It makes me wonder about her past. What do you know about her? Was she raised in a religious family?"

"Well, I know she has a couple of younger brothers and talks to her mom on the phone every few weeks. She goes home at Thanksgiving and Christmas. Her dad died a few years ago. I've never heard her mention going to church or anything like that."

Thinking about it, I realized that I hardly knew any more about Sylvia's family than I did about Alex's. Odd, since we had lived together for over a year now. Her mom lived somewhere in Michigan—Detroit I think—and had never been to Kentucky as far as I knew.

"I would be willing to bet she's had a religious upbringing," he said. "That might have a bearing on why she's so hostile toward anything about the church. She's rebelling against something."

After we hung up I stayed in my room awhile, thinking about what the preacher had said. I had no doubt Sylvia hated religion in any form, but why? And how did she know that stuff about David and Solomon?

The best way to find out was to ask her. I opened my door and went out into the living room, ready to put her through an inquisition. I wouldn't take no for an answer.

Too late. While I was talking on the phone, Sylvia had left the apartment.

"Clark and Hasna Building Company," I spoke into the speaker of my headset. Whenever I wore that thing I felt like a kid with orthodontic headgear, but it sure was convenient when I wanted to keep using my hands while I talked on the phone.

Alison had called in sick with a terrible headache and I was trying to do both jobs, so I was swamped. Mr. Clark had several letters he wanted in the mail before the close of business, and the monthly invoices were due to go out, too. In front of me lay a pile of incoming mail I hadn't had a chance to get to, and the phone just wouldn't stop ringing.

"May I speak with Mayla Strong?" asked a female voice on the other end.

"Speaking."

"Oh, Mayla, it's you. This is Marsha McDaniel from church."

I had never met her personally, but I had a vague idea she was a dark-haired woman who sang in the choir. I slit open an envelope and placed the letter in Mr. Hasna's correspondence file. "Hi, Marsha. What can I do for you?"

"Well, I wanted to talk to you about something new we're starting at church. It's a drama group. It's not going to be big, you know, just eight or ten people. We'll put together little skits or mini plays or monologues to perform during the worship service once a month or so. Lots of the big churches do it, so there's plenty of material out there to perform. Pastor Paul thought you might be interested."

"He did?" It must be an attempt on his part to find a place for me to serve. "Well, the only problem is that I'm in Lexington and I work most nights. When will you practice?"

"We haven't picked a time yet, but we're talking about Sunday afternoons, or maybe Wednesday nights. We're thinking we'll practice once a week to start, but then we won't have to get together that often except when we're actually performing a skit. Depending on how big the group is, not everyone would have a part every time. So really you could participate as often as you like, or only when you have time, or whatever."

It sounded pretty flexible. I could arrange to have a few Wednesdays or Sundays off at The Max. Jolene had not scheduled me to work on a Sunday since our discussion, not even a Sunday night. Fine with me. The tips weren't that good on Sunday nights anyway.

"I don't have any acting experience," I warned her.

"Not a problem. Experience is not required, just a willingness to learn. And we will memorize our lines, so if you can do that I'm sure you'll be fine."

"Well—" I wasn't feeling very enthusiastic about this, but if the preacher had suggested it, I figured maybe I should agree. "Okay. I'll give it a try."

"Great!" She sounded pleased. "We're planning an organizational meeting tomorrow night while the prayer meeting is going on. I have a skit I want to try, and we thought we could read through it and pick our parts. Can you make it?"

It just so happened that I wasn't scheduled to work the next day. I had planned to stay home and get some laundry done, but Sylvia had the night off, too. After our run-in, I was happy to have a reason to avoid the apartment as much as possible.

"Sure, I'll be there."

"See you then." I pressed the button to disconnect the call, an uneasy feeling nagging at me. I had never done any sort of acting, even in school. I auditioned once for a play in seventh grade, but I didn't make it and never tried again.

On the other hand, this was a new Mayla. The Bible said that God gives us all talents and gifts. Who knows? Maybe acting was one of my God-given talents. What better way to find out than to give it a try?

I had barely gotten my finger off the disconnect button when the phone rang again.

"Clark and Hasna Building Company."

"I have achieved the impossible," said Stuart's voice. "Thank me."

"Thank you," I replied. "What have you done?"

"I found Alex's family. Piece of cake. I got on the Internet and searched the public phone book listings. There are only three Markhams in Pikeville, and the first one on the list is Alexander Markham Sr. I figure it's a pretty safe bet that's his father."

"You think?" I asked sarcastically.

He sounded hurt. "Hey, give me some credit for creativity. You didn't think of searching the Internet."

He had me there. "Okay, okay, you are brilliant, Stuart. Thanks. Did you call them?"

"Are you nuts? They hate gays, remember?"

"How are they going to know you're gay over the phone?" I asked.

"I'm a guy, and I'm calling about Alex. They'll figure it out, and I just don't think I can handle it if they start yelling at me. I think you should call. After all, it was your idea."

I sighed. I didn't look forward to that conversation either. "Yeah, I guess you're right. What's the number?"

I wrote it down on a yellow sticky note and slapped it on my computer monitor so I would remember to take it home. "Thanks, Stuart."

"Let me know what they say. Oh, and by the way, here's a bit of news for you. According to a reliable rumor, Stephen went by the hospital last night and told Alex he's seeing someone else."

My hand formed into a fist and I had to stop myself from pounding on the desk. "Nice guy."

"Yeah, I know. Like I told you, he's not one of my favorite people. Anyway, I thought I would run by the hospital on my way home. Alex probably needs to see a friendly face."

"Maybe even two. I'll stop by on my way to The Max tonight," I promised.

"Catch you later," Stuart said, and the line clicked in my ear as he hung up.

I got back to work, but I had a sick feeling in the pit of my stomach thinking of Alex lying in that hospital bed with no one to visit him but a couple of people he didn't even know that well. He had been deserted by everyone he cared about—first his family, and now Stephen. It just wasn't fair.

Life's not fair, I heard Mama's voice repeating in my head. She had certainly told me that often enough after Daddy died. And she always continued, *but it goes on anyway. And so will we.*

Of course, that wouldn't be much comfort to Alex. Especially since for him the last part wasn't true.

I did stop by the hospital on the way to my night job, but Alex wasn't in the mood for visitors. He stared at the television and would only respond yes or no to my questions. I'm sure I would have been depressed, too, in his place. I had to hurry and get to work at The Max, so I didn't try too hard to pull him out of it. I left feeling just as depressed as he was.

I decided to call his parents on my break at eight o'clock. I went out to the parking lot and sat in my car so I would have a quiet place to talk, and made the call on my cell phone.

"Oh, Lord," I prayed before I punched the last number, "please help me say the right things."

Someone picked up on the third ring and a man's deep voice said, "Hello?"

I wasn't expecting him to sound so pleasant. "Uh, hello. My name is Mayla Strong. I'm looking for Alexander Markham."

"Well, you've found him. What can I do for you, Miss Strong?"

This was getting better all the time. He sounded really friendly. I started to feel a tiny glimmer of confidence. Maybe this wouldn't be so bad after all.

"Actually, Mr. Markham, I'm not calling for myself," I told him. "I'm a friend of Alex's."

After a long pause he said, "There's no one here by that name." The voice was decidedly less friendly than a moment before.

"I know that, because Alex is here. He's in the hospital, actually, and that's why I'm—"

"Stop right there," Mr. Markham demanded. "You've got the wrong number."

"Aren't you Alexander Markham, Alex's father?"

The voice that answered might have belonged to a completely different man, one so cold and distant that I felt chilled to the bone.

"I have no son."

I heard a click, and my cell phone was dead.

So much for contacting Alex's family.

Chapter 8

I enjoyed the drive to Salliesburg the following evening. My little Honda didn't have a great air conditioner, but it had been a cool summer day without much humidity so it felt good to ride along the curvy road with the windows down. Interstate 64 was a more direct route from Lexington to Salliesburg, and I always took that on Saturdays when I worked the late shift at the restaurant and then drove to Mama's house at night. But whenever I made the trip during the day, I took the back way through the country, especially in the summer. To me, that road represented the very best of Kentucky—rolling hills covered in deep green grass, tall trees with thick trunks and so heavy with leaves you couldn't see the branches, pastures dotted with grazing cattle, long dirt driveways with white farmhouses at the end. A few horses, of course, but this wasn't the rich Kentucky horse country. Plain farm people lived here, people who raised cows and chickens and planted fields full of tobacco or corn in neat, diagonal rows that went on as far as you could see.

My favorite part of the road was an old metal bridge that crossed over the Kentucky River about ten miles before you got to Salliesburg. When I was a kid, we called it the Singing Bridge because the tires made a musical hum as they rolled over it. Mama would hum in unison with the bridge, and at the other end I always applauded their duet.

I was in a great mood when I got to the church, refreshed and ready to try something new. A good number of cars were scattered around the parking lot, probably for some Bible study or other. I parked and went inside, looking around for a sign of the drama team meeting.

Instead, I found Mr. Holmes.

He lurked just inside the sanctuary doors, keeping an eagle eye focused on the entry hall. I didn't see him at first, but as I made my way toward the stairway leading down to the Sunday school rooms, he silently slipped out from the dark sanctuary and stepped right in front of me, blocking my path and scaring the daylights right out of me.

"Oh!" I shouted, startled. "You scared me. What the heck are you doing in there in the dark?"

His scowl deepened as he glared down on me from a height that seemed to increase with disapproval as he stared pointedly at my labret and nostril studs.

"Ain't never seen you here on Wednesdays," he growled, silently demanding an explanation for my presence at a time other than my regularly scheduled Sunday morning appearances.

I looked him dead in the face, weighing my answer. On the one hand, it was none of his business when and why I chose to come to church, and I was sorely tempted to tell him so. On the other hand, that probably wasn't the most Christian way to answer. So I bit my lip for a moment until I had enough control of my frustration to give him a bright smile.

"I'm joining the new church drama team. Any idea where they're meeting?"

His eyes narrowed and his gaze swept me from foot to scalp, an expression of clear disbelief on his face. My frustration flared into anger at his rudeness, and before I could stop I found myself snapping, "You don't have to be rude, you know. A simple answer would be just fine."

His eyebrows rose in surprise. He stood silent for a moment, then gave a snort and a shrug.

"Downstairs."

He turned away from me, as if he didn't consider me worth any more of his time, then slunk back into the dark sanctuary and left me standing alone in the entry hall. I stared at the dim shadow of his figure moving slowly down the center aisle in the darkness, his back rigid despite the stooped shoulders. It occurred to me suddenly that Mr. Holmes must have a sad life to be such a crank.

In the next moment, I shook myself. Sad? No way. I knew better. That grouchy old man was anything but sad; he was the most judgmental old creep I'd met in a long time. Shaking my head, I turned away and went down the stairs, looking for the drama team.

I found them in one of the Sunday school rooms downstairs.

"There you are, Mayla," said the dark-haired woman I had correctly guessed was Marsha. She wore an oversized tee shirt that said "*Fully Rely On God*" beneath a picture of a frog. Grabbing my arm, she pulled me into the room where they had folded up the long tables and leaned them against one wall, leaving the middle of the room empty. Seven or eight people sat in chairs lining the walls. "Everyone, this is Mayla."

A few of them stared at me with shocked expressions, and I knew they hadn't yet been close enough to me on Sunday mornings to see my hair or facial jewelry. Actually, I had changed my hair color just the weekend before. Instead of Egyptian Plum, I had chosen a shade called Black Cherry, and I wore a tiny little stud in my nostril with a stone that matched the color almost exactly. I still wore the cross below my bottom lip.

"Hi, everyone," I said with a little wave. Some mumbled greetings, and several gave me genuine smiles of welcome.

"I'm expecting a few more people," Marsha said, handing me a package of stapled papers, "but I think we should go ahead and get started."

She stood at one end of the room and put an official-looking smile on her face.

"Welcome, everyone, to the first meeting of the SICC drama team. I'm thrilled you could all make it, and I'm confident this is going to be a lot of fun. The script I've given you is one I selected to try as our first, because it has lots of parts and I thought our first skit should be one in which we all participate."

I looked down at the script. The cover page proclaimed the title: "Life's Too Short." I flipped to the next page and looked at the list of characters. There were a bunch.

Marsha was still talking. "We can delete several of the characters without hurting the message, so we can adapt it to fit our size. Why don't we all take a moment to read through it and see which characters jump out at us."

I glanced through the predictable little story about a woman who dies and goes to heaven. She talks to several of the people there and finally discovers that she needs to have a formal letter of introduction from Jesus in order to stay. She doesn't have it, so she gets kicked out, and as expected, wakes up the next morning completely reformed. I didn't see a single part that jumped out at me as one I would want to do.

"You should play the lead, Marsha," said the slim, blonde woman sitting next to me.

"Well, of course we want to be fair," fluttered Marsha, clearly pleased and clearly intending to take the lead even if no one had suggested it. "Is there anyone else who would like to read for the part of Shirley?"

No one said a word.

"I have been rehearsing that part," Marsha confided, "so if no one objects . . ."

No one objected.

"Okay, then that's settled. Who's next? Phil, which part would you like to play?"

Phil, one of three men in the group, screwed his face up as he considered. "I like the scene with the guy who has the letter. I could probably do that one."

Marsha beamed. "That's exactly what I had in mind. And Randy, I thought you would be perfect for the man with the banjo. Would that be okay with you?"

Randy shrugged one shoulder and then nodded.

"Good. Now, Mayla," she turned to me, "I wondered if you might like to play the part of the guide."

I swallowed. "The guide? That's a pretty big part, and remember what I said about having no acting experience."

"Nonsense," Marsha said, "most of us don't have any experience. In fact, I think I'm the only one who has ever done any acting, and of course I've acted in several semiprofessional plays, though it has been a few years."

She ducked her head in a self-effacing manner, and I had a sneaking, if uncharitable, suspicion that the entire drama group was nothing more than a plot to give Marsha the opportunity to perform before a captive audience. A dozen excuses for backing out of the whole thing ran through my mind, but in the end I remembered what Pastor Paul had said—that finding a place to serve was a way to grow in my Christian walk. So instead of backing out, I smiled and said, "Okay, I'll give it a shot."

"Wonderful." Marsha beamed as she turned to give the next person her assignment.

I took the opportunity to read over my part. I probably should have been flattered; next to Marsha's, I had been given the second biggest part. I would play the angel guide, who meets Marsha at the pearly gates and walks her through heaven, introduces her to various people, and wisely explains all the things she needs to learn. I would be onstage most of the time. It would take some memorizing, but I thought I could handle it.

I turned my attention back to Marsha, who had finished assigning parts to her satisfaction and was walking into the center of the room.

"Let's see, we're going to need a few props," she said. "Most of the time, we will perform without props, but for our first skit I think we should have a few visuals. Let's have a couple of chairs over here to represent the pearly gates, and then we'll walk this way through heaven." She indicated a diagonal path from the door to the back corner of the room.

When the chairs had been arranged to Marsha's satisfaction, everyone else sat down and the two of us stepped out into the hall. We were to walk through the doorway, with me lead-

ing Marsha, and head toward the pearly gates. As we encoun-
tered the residents of heaven, each of them would stand up and
take their place in our path.

"Okay, is everyone ready? Then let's go, Mayla."

The part of the angel guide reminded me of the three ghost
guides in *A Christmas Carol,* and I decided that a little Dickens
flavor would be just the thing. We stood in the doorway and
Marsha grabbed my arm, ready to be guided into heaven. I did
my best to put a haunting inflection into my voice as I read
from the script.

"Greetings, Shirley, and welcome to heaven. I am here to
guide you, for there are people you must meet. Take my arm
and let us walk together."

I took a step forward through the doorway, but Marsha
didn't move. Instead she stood looking at me with something
like alarm on her face. I noticed several open-mouthed stares
around the room.

"Uh, Mayla," she said, "what's that voice?"

"I figured it would sound good. Sort of heavenly."

Marsha frowned. "It sounds more like a ghost than an
angel. I think you should just talk normally."

So much for creativity. I shrugged and backed up to try it
again. This time I used my normal voice. But again, when it
came time to step into the room to approach the pearly gates,
Marsha stood stock still, as if her feet were nailed to the floor.

"That's a touch too dry," she said, a frown creasing her
forehead. "Can't you put some life into it?"

Huh?

"You said to talk like I normally do. That's how I talk."

"Yes, but now you sound too earthly. We need something a
little more here. Like maybe a little inflection in your voice, a
little emotion. Can you do that?"

I nodded, and did it again. This time I put emotion into my voice. I put inflection. I sounded as angel-like as I could.

Apparently it didn't come off well. I actually heard some snickers from inside the room, but of course I couldn't see who was laughing, because I was out in the hallway. A feeling crept up inside me that this was not going to turn out to be my place of service after all. I was not having fun.

Neither was Marsha.

"Mayla, you and I will have to work on this later." Her voice was decidedly chilly. "For now, let's just get through the skit once, and then we'll see where we need to go from there."

She took my arm and we walked through the doorway, stopping just inside the room. She stared at the two chairs, looked upward dramatically and said in a voice full of emotion and loaded with inflection, "These are the pearly gates, and look! They're really made of pearl! They're so beautiful."

She stopped, and there was a long silence. Everyone was staring at me, and I realized the next line was mine. Shuffling my script, I found my part and replied, with feeling, "Only those who have been invited can step through them and onto the streets of gold. Come. There are people you must meet."

I tried to imitate her, but even I could hear that it didn't sound the same coming from me. Marsha closed her eyes and breathed a heavy sigh, as if the weight of the world had been placed on her shoulders.

We took a step forward to pass the pearly gates, Marsha's hand on my arm, me guiding her beside the chairs. I don't know how it happened, but maybe I was nervous from my obvious failure at script reading. Somehow my foot got tangled in one of the chair legs, and before I could stop myself, I tripped over the "pearly gates" and tumbled to the ground. Reflex made me grab at Marsha for support as I went down.

She sort of bounced off the other chair before she hit the floor right beside me.

That caused quite a commotion. People rushed forward to help us up, and I found myself being lifted into the hastily righted chair. Someone asked if anything was broken, and the skinny blonde lady wondered aloud if she should call 9-1-1. Marsha replied sharply—and with plenty of emotion—that we were fine and would everyone please go back to their seats.

Of course I was embarrassed and apologized to Marsha several times, but she insisted that I shouldn't worry, no harm done, and she wanted to try it again from the beginning.

I'm sure the only reason I ran into the doorjamb as I headed toward the hallway was because I was flustered and wasn't paying attention. My head hit the wood with a loud smack and it hurt. I actually saw stars. Marsha and the others rushed to my side again, and though I kept assuring everyone I felt fine, they insisted that I sit down while someone ran to get me a glass of water. Humiliated, I prayed silently for an opportunity to sneak out of the room unnoticed.

As I drank my water and cursed myself for ever agreeing to do such a ridiculous thing as act in a drama group, Marsha had a quick conversation in the hallway with Randy, the banjo man. She came back into the room and perched on one of the "pearly gates" next to me.

"Uh, Mayla, I was just talking to Randy, and you know what? He has some acting experience, too."

"He does?" I asked, spying a possible escape.

"Yes, and I was thinking . . . since the angel guide is such a big part, maybe we should let him try it this first time. Perhaps you would do better with a smaller part, at least this once, and then in our next skit we can expand you into a larger role."

"That sounds like a good plan," I said, relieved. "What part did you have in mind?"

"Well," Marsha said, not meeting my gaze directly, "we thought maybe you could play a guard."

"A guard." I glanced up at Randy, who looked hard at something off in the distance. "I don't remember a guard in the script."

"Well, there isn't one, but that's the fun thing about this script. We can do whatever we want with it. And we were thinking, since the angel guide says that you can only get through the pearly gates with an invitation, wouldn't you think there should be an angel guard there to make sure no one slips through?"

It sounded logical. "What would I do?"

"Just guard. Stand there by the gates, and as Shirley and the guide go by, you watch them pass."

"I wouldn't say anything?"

"No, but that's something we can work toward next time."

"I see."

I did see, too. I was terrible at script reading, I couldn't get the right emotion in my voice, and I was a klutz besides. What better role than to have me *stand* there through the entire skit, unmoving and silent.

Of course I agreed. I wasn't stupid, and I had made a big enough fool of myself for one night. I certainly wasn't in a hurry to repeat the effort in front of the entire congregation. Mama would die of embarrassment. So I obediently stood by the pearly gates the rest of the night, trying to look like a guard and trying not to move.

I have to admit the others were pretty good. I thought the drama group would end up being a good thing for the church.

But definitely without me.

✝

If you can believe it, the night got worse before it got better. When I arrived home, I found my mail in a neat pile on my bed, like it always was when Sylvia got there before I did. On top of the usual pile of junk mail and credit card offers lay a cream-colored envelope with my name and address in small, neat handwriting. The return address label had colorful little flowers bordering the name, Louise Strong. My Aunt Louise. I had not seen her since my father's funeral and had only a vague memory of an immaculately dressed woman with soft blonde hair and a worried expression. My heart beat a little faster when I saw that the address was my grandmother's house in Orlando. I ripped open the envelope and flattened out the crisp sheet of folded stationery inside.

Dear Mayla,

I know you weren't expecting to get a letter from me, but I was certainly happy to read yours. Not a week has gone by that I haven't prayed for you and your mother. Has she become a Christian, too? Please convey my greetings to her as well.

I wish I could say I was writing on behalf of your grandmother, but I'm afraid that would be untrue. She has become a very bitter woman in the past twelve years, Mayla. Her health has deteriorated, too, which is why I moved home to care for her a few years ago. She never quite recovered from your father's death, you see, and I'm afraid she still blames your mother. At first I tried to talk to her about it. I told her that Angela did the only thing she could, and that no doubt she suffered to make that decision. But every time we talked, Mother became enraged and I worried about her heart, so I stopped discussing it with her.

I thought your letter might be just the thing after all these years to help her get beyond her anger, but I'm afraid it only brought everything to the surface again, and she had another spell with her heart. I don't know if anything can ever soften her.

I know this is not what you wanted to hear, and I'm sorry. Pray for her, Mayla. Sometimes she is harsh, but she is my mother, and your grandmother, and I love her.

Love,
Aunt Louise

I sat on the bed and read the letter again, my throat tightening around a lump of sobs that threatened to pour out. I had so hoped . . .

I refolded the single sheet of cream-colored paper and put it carefully back in the ripped envelope, which I placed in the drawer of my bedside table. It didn't matter what I had hoped about my grandmother. It obviously wasn't going to happen. But Aunt Louise was right about one thing—I could pray for her. And I would, beginning at that very moment.

As I did, I felt the tightness in my throat ease, and the ache in my heart dulled as I poured out my feelings to God.

The ringing of the phone jolted me out of a deep sleep. In my confusion, I reached for the alarm clock and punched vainly at the snooze button. Then my eyes focused on the red block numbers—eleven fifty-two. Almost midnight. I grabbed the phone as it began its second ring, then realized it was my cell phone ringing. Fumbling for my purse on the floor beside my bed, I finally managed to answer the call.

"Hello," I said groggily, struggling to wake up.

"Uh, hello," a voice whispered. "Is this Marla Strong?"

"It's *Mayla* Strong," I replied.

"Sorry, I thought it was a mistake. I never heard of anyone named Mayla."

"Yeah, I get that a lot." I rubbed my eyes and yawned. "So who is this?"

The answer brought me instantly awake.

"My name is Lindsey Markham. I'm Alex's sister."

I sat straight up in bed. "Alex's sister," I repeated. "I didn't know he had a sister."

"Well, we haven't talked in a while. He probably doesn't even remember my name. But I'm his sister."

It finally registered in my sleep-addled brain that the whispering voice sounded pretty young.

"Let me guess," I said. "Your dad's asleep and doesn't know you're calling."

"Yeah," she admitted. "He'd go ballistic if he knew. I heard him talking to you last night and I got your number off the Caller ID so I could call you back. I couldn't hear much, but I did hear Daddy say he didn't have a son. We haven't heard from Alex since I was little, so I had to call and find out how he is. Are you a friend of his? Is he okay?"

I answered with a question of my own. "How old are you, Lindsey?"

"I'm fifteen," she said, and from the touch of defiance in her voice I could almost picture a determined chin tilted upward as she said it. Fifteen wasn't as young as I had feared. I hesitated, wondering if she knew that Alex was gay. I certainly didn't want to "out" him to his own sister.

"Well," I said slowly, "I actually called to tell your dad that Alex is in the hospital."

"Is it serious?"

"It could be," I said, not wanting to commit but also not wanting to make light of Alex's condition.

There was a pause before she asked in a voice even quieter than before, "Is it AIDS?"

She knew.

"Yes," I admitted, "it is. And it's pretty bad, Lindsey." There was a long silence, and I was afraid she might be crying. "Lindsey?"

"Is he going to die?"

I took a deep breath. I was treading on thin ice here. It was one thing to try to convince a grown man to speak to his gay son, but quite another to break the news to a teenager that her big brother would soon die of AIDS.

"It's very bad," I said, unwilling to say more.

"Does he have someone to take care of him?"

"Not really," I told her. "There's the hospital staff and a few friends like me, but no one special. No family." I winced as the last words crossed my lips.

There was a pause, and then Lindsey said in a calm voice, "I get it. Your area code is 859, so I know you're in Kentucky. What town? What hospital is he in?"

"We're in Lexington, and he's at Saint Patrick's Hospital, room 347."

"Okay, when are visiting hours? I'm coming tomorrow."

Holy cow! What had I done?

"You're what? How? What will your father say?"

"Lexington isn't that far, just three hours or so. My boy-friend has a car, and we can ditch school for a day. He'll drive me up. As for what Daddy will say, I don't plan to tell him."

She sounded just like me at fifteen. Mama and I had been close, but she would have been stunned if she had known all the stuff I did when I was supposed to be at school. Someday I'll confess it all to her. Maybe.

"Well, before you get here you should know that Alex didn't want me to call your parents, and he doesn't know I did. He'll probably be mad at me."

"Tough," Lindsey said, sounding even more like me. "He'll get over it. I'm coming whether he likes it or not. I want to see my big brother."

Her voice broke on the last word, and I could hear her struggling not to cry. I couldn't imagine how she felt, but I was thankful that Alex had someone who loved him whether he was gay or not. A thought occurred to me, and I spoke quickly before I could seriously consider whether or not helping a fifteen-year-old ditch school would be considered "contribut-ing to the delinquency of a minor" in a court of law.

"I'm really glad to hear you say that, Lindsey. Listen, take my number with you and call me when you get into town. If you want, I can meet you somewhere and take you over there."

"I would really like that," she said, relief saturating her voice. She wasn't as tough as she let on, and that didn't surprise me either. We rarely are.

"All right then, I'll talk to you tomorrow."

"Good-bye."

I pressed the End button and immediately dialed Stuart's number. I knew it was late, but I just had to tell someone, and I knew Stuart would share my excitement that someone from Alex's family was going to visit.

"That's great, Mayla," he said sleepily when I told him the news. "Really. Tomorrow I'll be thrilled. Right now, I'm asleep, and I don't know if you're real or just a really vivid dream. If you're real, tell me again in the morning, right after I bawl you out for waking me up in the middle of the night."

It took me a second to realize that Stuart had hung up on me.

Well, maybe excitement was a little too much to expect after midnight.

Chapter 9

At eleven o'clock the next morning, Lindsey called to let me know that she and her boyfriend had arrived in Lexington and were hanging out by the rocking chairs on the porch of the Cracker Barrel at Exit 115. I grabbed my purse, told Alison I'd be back after lunch, and drove out to meet them.

As I walked up to the Cracker Barrel, I saw approval in both sets of eyes when they got a good look at me. Some teenagers see facial piercing as a sort of acceptance criteria. I could see they hadn't expected someone like me, but I'm used to that; I am rarely what people expect.

Lindsey Markham looked like her brother. Actually, she looked like what I imagined Alex had looked like before the disease robbed him of his hair, the color in his cheeks, and about forty pounds. Lindsey's eyes were the same hazel color, and she had the same straight nose, only daintier and feminine. Her thick, dark hair was pulled into a ponytail, and she kept nervously pulling out the scrunchee and putting it back in. She also bounced on her toes a lot, another nervous gesture that one of the cheerleaders at my high school used to do constantly. In fact, Lindsey had that wholesome look that reminded me of high school cheerleaders, and it wasn't much of a stretch to imagine her in a short skirt with pom-poms, shouting, "Go Team!" It made me a little sad to see her looking so robust in her teenage health and to think that Alex had once looked like her.

"Lindsey, right?" I asked.

She bounced on her toes and nodded. "Yeah, and you're Mayla? This is Dirk."

Dirk was a typical high school rebel—longish hair, not too clean, ripped tee shirt with a pack of cigarettes sticking out of the breast pocket, silver hoop earrings in both ears. Not that I have anything against pierced ears on men or women, but my first thought was that Lindsey's father was probably beside himself with fury at the thought of his little girl going out with this guy. If he even knew, that is.

Dirk ducked his head, looking away as he fumbled for a cigarette. I nodded in his direction and focused my attention on Lindsey.

"Listen, remember what I said last night? Alex doesn't know you're coming, and he probably won't be too happy with either one of us when he sees you. Don't take it personally, okay?"

I had been worried about that. She was his kid sister, after all, and if he got really upset, he might throw her out. And if it was the last time she ever saw him . . . I just didn't want to be responsible for any permanent emotional scars that would send her into therapy later in life.

She gave a brief, nervous smile, which was quickly erased. "Don't worry about it. I'm a big girl, and I can handle my brother."

I believed her. And on second thought, given my brief exposure to her father, she probably already had plenty of stuff for the therapists without me.

I waited until they got into their car, an old Dodge Caravan with almost bald tires, rust eating away at the body, and smoke belching out of the tailpipe. They followed me downtown, my windows rattling from the bass on Dirk's stereo whenever we stopped at a light. I have been in many a car with a hot stereo, and this was the first time it ever irritated me. It seemed so shallow to be playing the stereo like that when you're driving your girlfriend to visit her dying brother in the hospital. *Gosh, I must be getting old!*

We parked side by side in the parking lot. Lindsey looked really nervous, and she rearranged her ponytail at least four times during the short walk to the revolving door at the main entrance. I didn't know exactly how she felt, but I can tell you I was pretty nervous too. Dirk was the only one who didn't appear ready to bolt. He puffed furiously on a cigarette before stubbing it out in the ashtray outside the entrance.

My stomach gave a little flutter when the elevator doors opened and I stepped out into the hall. Seated at the nurses' station, Gail bent over the desk as she wrote on a pad of paper. She glanced up briefly, and her head jerked up as she caught sight of me and then Lindsey. Standing so quickly that her chair went rolling across the floor behind her, she came around the high counter and approached us.

"Are you a friend of Alex's?" she asked, her gaze taking in every feature of Lindsey's face and drawing the obvious conclusion before the girl answered.

"I'm his sister," Lindsey told her, bouncing nervously on her toes. "This is my boyfriend, Dirk."

Gail smiled at them both. "I'm so glad you've come, and I'm sure Alex will be, too. I just came from his room, so I know he's awake and ready for visitors. Let me know if I can answer any questions or bring you anything."

Lindsey nodded, and Dirk fidgeted with a silver ring on his left hand, twirling it around with his thumb.

"Alex's room is over here," I said, forcing myself to walk quickly before I chickened out and left Lindsey to go in alone.

At the door, I paused and said in a low voice, "Let me go in first and prepare him."

Lindsey nodded, her gaze fixed on the curtain pulled closed in the room behind me, trying to get a glimpse of the person on the other side. I had no idea what I was going to say, but I felt like I owed it to Alex to confess before springing Lindsey on him. I stepped into the room and said in a normal voice, "Hey Alex, you decent in there?"

"Hey, Mayla. Sure. C'mon in."

He sounded tired, and when I stepped around the curtain I tried to look at him with fresh eyes, seeing him as Lindsey would one minute from now. If he had looked weak when I first met him, now he looked frail and utterly fragile, as if any physical effort at all might finally zap the last of his energy and finish him. The ugly sores on his forehead stood out starkly on the sheet-white skin, and his lips were gray. But his eyes, the same color as his sister's, held warmth and friendship when he greeted me.

I hoped they would still look the same a few minutes from now.

"Uh, Alex, I've got a surprise for you," I began.

"Oh? Another of your stories? I could use a good laugh today."

"Well, it's not a story exactly, but I do have something to tell you. Remember last week when I asked about your family?"

His smile faded, and I rushed on, not stopping for breath. "I know you told me to drop it, and I know it was none of my business, but you're my friend and I care about you, and I really felt like your family should know, and I got Stuart to help me find them, and then I called them and there's someone here who wants to see you."

There. I had implicated Stuart, too, and I hadn't intended to do that, but it tumbled out before I could think about it. Then, before Alex could react, Lindsey stepped around the curtain to stand beside me at the foot of his bed.

She stood very still, and I glanced at her face long enough to see some pretty obvious emotions displayed there: shock, pain, compassion, anger—at her father, maybe?—and finally, to my relief, an unbelievable tenderness and love. I looked at Alex and saw the love mirrored behind a pool of tears that filled up and overflowed, running in unrestrained rivers down his face. And then my own eyes became rivers, too, and I couldn't see anything.

"Big brother," whispered Lindsey, swallowing hard and smiling.

"Little sister," he responded, and his tears flowed faster as his eyes drank in the sight of her. Maybe I imagined it, but his voice sounded a little stronger, as if just seeing Lindsey gave him strength he hadn't had a moment before.

"Well," I said after a few long seconds, during which I stood there awkwardly, a forgotten outsider witnessing an intensely personal family moment, "I'll just leave you two to visit."

I left, though I doubt they noticed. I passed Dirk in the hallway. He was leaning against the wall several feet from Alex's door, twirling his ring and looking completely out of. place. I stopped to say good-bye to him.

"Can you find your way back to Pikeville?" I asked.

"Yeah, no problem."

I smiled and started to walk on, but he stopped me. "So Lindsey says this dude is gonna die, right?"

"'Fraid so."

"Will it be, like, soon?"

I lifted my shoulders. "Hard to tell, but it looks like it could be soon."

He glanced quickly at the door. "It's not, like, contagious or anything, is it? I mean, Lindsey's gonna be okay in there, ain't she?"

I looked closely at him, wondering if he was worried more about himself or Lindsey. He looked genuinely concerned, and I didn't think it was for selfish reasons. I decided his question could be taken at face value—he wanted some assurance of Lindsey's safety. Maybe he really cared for her.

"She'll be fine," I assured him. "She can't catch what he has."

He nodded, relieved, and leaned back against the wall, apparently prepared to wait for Lindsey as long as she wanted to stay. I raised my hand in farewell and walked away, listening to the murmur of Lindsey's and Alex's quiet voices drifting into the hallway behind me. As I passed the nurse's station, Gail gave me a huge grin and a thumbs-up.

As my car rolled down the exit driveway from the parking lot, my cell phone rang. I fished in my purse blindly, one hand on the steering wheel, my right rear tire bumping up on the curb when I turned into the street. An old woman walking on the sidewalk glared at me and pointedly made a wide detour onto the grass in the opposite direction from my car. Cell phones and automobiles are definitely not a safe combination.

The number was one I didn't recognize, but the area code was Salliesburg.

"Hello?" I asked, fumbling for the earpiece as I stopped at a traffic light.

"Is this Marla Strong?" asked an unfamiliar female voice.

"Yes, this is *Mayla* Strong. Who is this?"

"My name is Faye Roberts. I'm a nurse at Salliesburg Regional Medical Center, and I'm calling about your mother."

Have you ever heard someone say that their heart skipped a beat? I never believed it—I always thought it was just a figure of speech that people used when describing something really frightening—but I'm here to tell you, I was wrong. My heart really did miss a beat, or at least that's what it felt like to me.

"Mama?" I croaked. "What's wrong with Mama?"

"She's fine," the woman's voice told me, "or at least, she's going to be fine. But she had an accident at work and broke her foot. She's waiting to have it casted right now, and the doctor has decided to keep her overnight to be sure everything's okay. She wanted me to give you a call."

Keep her overnight? For a broken foot?

"Can I talk to her?"

"Well, not right at the moment, because we've just called for an orderly to wheel her up to orthopedics, but if you call back in about an hour the front desk can transfer you directly to her room. I can give you the number if you have a pencil."

"Never mind," I told her, "I can be there by then. I'm on my way."

I pressed the End button and sat there, hands on the steering wheel, willing my heartbeat to slow down. Mama in the hospital! My stomach tightened at the thought. Mama was never sick; she was one of the most active people I knew. I couldn't imagine her having the patience to tolerate the restrictions of a broken foot, much less a stay in the hospital.

A car behind me honked and I realized the light had turned green some time ago. I raised my hand in acknowledgment and stomped on the gas. I kept telling myself I had plenty of time, that everything was fine, but some irrational form of panic kept whispering that I had to get to Salliesburg immediately, that I had to be with Mama. I couldn't stand the thought of her lying alone, shivering in one of those thin hospital gowns on a rolling gurney in a deserted hallway, waiting for an orderly to come get her and take her to orthopedics. What if they forgot about her? She could lie there for hours. Was she in pain? What if the pain got to be so terrible that she fainted—would anyone notice? Salliesburg was a small town, after all. What sort of care would she get in a small-town hospital? Did they even have real nurses there? Or did they just hire the local high school dropout because she went all the way through rehab and needed a job? For all I knew, a delinquent was taking care of my mama, dressed like a nurse and working in that little podunk hospital because she was cheaper than a real RN.

I would rescue Mama, that's what I'd do. I'd bring her up here to St. Patrick's—now *that* was a hospital where they knew how to take care of people. They had quality people on staff at St. Patrick's, people who cared, people like Nurse Gail.

My thoughts raced along, picking up speed and generally working me into a state of near panic as my Honda zoomed down the interstate. That the Lord sets His angels around us was proven that day by the fact that I made it without hurting

myself or anyone else, because I can honestly say I never noticed
I was driving. My car must have been on autopilot, because it
drove the thirty-five miles from Lexington to Salliesburg with
no help from the driver's seat.

It seemed like only minutes after I hung up my cell phone
that I pulled into the emergency room parking lot of the hospital. I grabbed my purse and raced for the automatic doors,
banging hard into them when they didn't open quickly enough.
I ran for the desk, where a woman in pink hospital scrubs sat
behind a computer monitor.

"Angela Strong," I shouted as she looked up at me, startled.
"Where is she?"

"Uh, they just took her up to a room a little while ago. Let
me see which one."

She nervously tapped out a request on her keyboard while
I bounced up and down very much like Lindsey had just an
hour before. The woman kept glancing up at me and quickly
looking away.

"Here it is. She's in room 204, bed B."

"Which way?" I asked, surprised to hear my voice come out
in a shout that made her flinch.

"Down that hallway to the main elevators, then turn left
on the second floor. And please, Miss, keep your voice down."

I ran the way she had indicated—literally ran like a
sprinter. People stared at me, and some of them moved out of
my way, flattening themselves against the corridor walls and
watching in astonishment as I raced by. I jabbed the elevator
button, and when the doors didn't open instantly, I looked
frantically around for another way. I found it—a gray metal
door marked "Stairs." I dashed up the steps three at a time and
burst out onto the second floor, startling an old man leaning
heavily on a walker with one hand and clutching his hospital

gown closed with the other. Ignoring him, I zoomed down the hallway in the direction of room 204. Grabbing the doorjamb to slow myself down, I catapulted into Mama's room. As my eyes took in the scene, I stopped short, staring in confusion and panting like an expectant mother practicing Lamaze.

Like Alex's room at St. Patrick's, the first bed, the one closest to the door, was empty. But Alex's room had never been so full of people! At first glance, I thought there must be at least ten, but a second look revealed only four, all of whom had turned to look at me with varying degrees of curiosity. A pretty redheaded nurse stood beside Mama's bed, holding a plastic cup with a bendable straw up to Mama's lips. Mr. Satterly, Mama's boss from the grocery store, stood at the foot of the bed holding a huge vase full of flowers, with two gigantic Mylar balloons hovering above his head. The third visitor, a lady I didn't recognize, stood on the other side of the bed holding a gold foil candy box. And amid them all was Mama, propped up on about a dozen pillows, wearing a lacy housecoat, covered in a fuzzy white blanket and looking for all the world like a queen being attended by her servants.

"There you are, Mayla," she said, completely unsurprised to see me, as if I had just stepped in from the next room. "Could you hand me my purse, sweetie? It's in that closet over there."

Stunned into silence, at least for the moment, I went obediently to the closet and retrieved Mama's purse—a straw number with big yellow sunflowers stuck all over it—from the clear plastic bag the hospital had put it in. I walked toward her as she took a dainty sip from the straw the nurse held to her lips. Taking the purse, she smiled up at me, then pulled out a bit of paper with her cramped handwriting all over it.

"While I was waitin' down in the emergency room, I made a list of a few things I need from home, if you don't mind.

Except I don't need the gown anymore, since Connie from the church was nice enough to bring me this beautiful new one." She fingered the lacy collar and dimpled with pleasure. "Feel it. It's so soft you can hardly believe it."

"But—but—how?" I stammered. "You just got here!"

"Well, I've been here for a couple of hours at least. And after all, Salliesburg *is* a small town. Edna here was kind enough to call Connie to start the prayer chain, and Connie rushed right out to bring me those flowers," she indicated a colorful splash of blossoms on the windowsill, "and this nightgown."

Edna, holding the chocolates, nodded in my direction. I noticed in passing that she was trying very hard not to stare at my lower lip, and as a result her gaze kept fixing itself on my nostril stud. I ignored her.

The nurse put the cup on a narrow bedside table with wheels, just like the one in Alex's room. The thought flew briefly through my mind that hospital supply clerks everywhere must order from the same catalog, because everything in the room looked just like Alex's.

"Now Mrs. Strong," the nurse said, "I'll leave and let you enjoy your visitors for a few more minutes, but then you really should rest."

Over Mama's head she gave the three of us a stern look and left the room. Mr. Satterly went to the windowsill and placed his flowers beside the other ones.

"We don't wanna keep you from your restin', Angela," he said, and I thought his smile looked a bit nervous. "Now don't you worry 'bout a thing. Worker's Comp's gonna cover everything, seein' as how it happened at the store and all. Just plain stupid, that's what them stock boys are."

He shook his head.

"Exactly what did happen?" I asked, giving him my most direct look. I can be pretty intimidating to people who aren't used to me. Poor Mr. Satterly's eyes widened, and he suddenly looked a lot more nervous.

"That's what I'm gonna find out," he said so intensely that it sound like a vow. "We got rules against piling them boxes up more than two high, so there was no cause to have them napkin cartons stacked four deep. No cause a'tall."

"Napkins?" I looked at Mama. "A box of napkins broke your foot?"

"*Feminine* napkins," Edna corrected, and Mr. Satterly's face pinked up. "They must have been stacked uneven, though, because Angela wasn't even going for them. She was reaching for a box of cash register tape on the shelf beside them and they toppled right over on her. It was pure bad luck that she grabbed the metal shelves on her way down and pulled them over, too. We heard her yelling all the way up front."

Mama sat there looking frail at the recounting of her trauma, though I began to suspect she was enjoying all the excitement more than she let on. Still, when I looked at her closely, I saw new lines around her mouth, and her eyes weren't quite as bright as usual. The crease between her eyebrows was deeper than ever. She looked like she did when she had one of her terrible headaches, so I figured she was in pain even if she did happen to be enjoying the attention. She wore a brave smile as she nodded good-bye to Mr. Satterly and Edna.

When they had gone, I perched on the edge of her bed, careful not to jiggle her too much, and we sat in silence a moment, watching each other.

"You okay?" I asked in a low voice. "I was really worried. I didn't even call work—just left and came here as fast as I could."

She patted my hand. "No need to worry, sweetie. I'm gonna be fine. The doctor said so. Old bones break easier than young ones, I guess."

I ignored the "old bones" comment. Since I had turned eighteen, she had been complaining to any and all about how she was getting old. She wasn't even fifty years old yet, so very few of her friends gave her any sympathy on that account.

"Then why do you have to stay in the hospital?"

She shrugged. "The doctor said he wanted to be sure I didn't suffer any delayed shock, or somethin' like that. Just a precaution, he said."

She snuggled back further into the cushion of the pillows. "I plan to enjoy myself. I got a remote control TV, and one of them cable channels has a marathon of *The Andy Griffith Show* goin' on. I'm gonna let them bring me dinner and eat in bed, and I can't remember the last time I did that."

She lowered her voice. "Though truth be told, I do feel kind of foolish, breaking my foot on somethin' as silly as a box of maxi pads. Thought I'd seen the last of those things when I had my hysterectomy five years ago."

Now that sounded like Mama! I laughed with relief, feeling the worry seep away when her tinkling laughter joined mine. At that moment, old Dr. Hopkins, Mama's family physician since she'd moved to Salliesburg, came through the door.

"Just as I thought," he said sternly, eyeing us over the top of his half glasses. "There's not a thing wrong with you, Angela Strong. What do you mean, disrupting my schedule like this, pulling me away from a waiting room full of patients to come over here and see you lazing around in bed in the middle of the day? A case of playing hooky if I ever saw one."

"That's just what I told those emergency room people, Doctor, but they wouldn't listen to me." Mama flashed her dimples. "But since they did get you out of that drab old office, maybe you can use me as an excuse to get in a few holes out at the country club before you go back."

Dr. Hopkins grinned. "Now there's an idea!" He carried a folder with some papers in it, and he sat on the edge of the empty bed to read through them. "Says here the break is a pretty clean one, along the left side of your foot. They already casted it?"

Mama leaned over to pull back the covers, exposing an old-fashioned plaster cast from her foot to just below her knee. Her toenails peeked out the end, polished with her favorite shiny pink.

"Hurt much?" he asked.

Mama hesitated. "A bit," she admitted, "but not as much as I would have thought a broken foot would hurt. More like a dull throbbing."

"That's because of the area of the break. It's in the fifth metatarsal. Not many nerves down there, and not many blood vessels either. That's good when you consider it won't hurt as much as a break somewhere else would, but bad when it comes to healing. Takes a long time to heal properly because of the insufficient blood supply, and in the meantime it doesn't take much to break it again. What did they tell you about your recovery?"

"They said I'd be off it for a week at least, no weight on it. And then I'd be in this cast for another month before they x-ray it again to see how it's goin'."

Dr. Hopkins nodded. "You listen to them. No weight at all, or you'll interfere with the bone repair your body is going to try to do. You're probably going to need some help for a few days, till you get used to navigating around with crutches."

He shifted his gaze toward me and gave me a hard stare over the top of those glasses. I thought of all the things sitting on my desk at the construction office waiting to be done, and of Jolene's face when I told her I needed a few days off from serving at The Max. Then I looked at Mama and thought of her trying to struggle up and down the stairs to go to the bathroom without help.

"Not a problem," I assured the doctor. "I've got some time off coming."

"Good." He closed the folder and stood up. "Angela, you just lie back and rest tonight. They've given you 800 mg of Tylenol, but I'll leave a prescription for something stronger if you need it. I'll call in the morning to see how you're doing, and you'll be home before lunch."

"Why does she have to stay here tonight?" I asked, still suspicious that they were keeping something more serious from me.

Dr. Hopkins shrugged. "A precaution only. She did take quite a fall, and her blood pressure was a touch high, probably from all the excitement. We need to be sure she doesn't start showing signs of other internal injuries. Unlikely, but it doesn't hurt to be cautious." He paused for a moment. "If you want my opinion, I think it's because the hospital wants to gouge Worker's Comp for as much as they can."

Grinning, he left the room.

"Now Mayla," Mama began as soon as he was out of sight, "you don't have to take off work. I'll be just fine by myself, and I'm sure my friends will stop by to check on me and lend a hand if I need them to. You've got your jobs, and bills to pay, and you can't afford to be takin' time off."

I stood. "Forget it. I'm going to stay with you for a few days, and you can just stop arguing about it. Now I'm going to run over to the house and get the things on this list, and I'll drop them by here on my way back to Lexington. Then I'll be back in the morning to take you home."

In my car, I prayed as I pulled out of the hospital parking lot. "Thanks, Lord, for being with Mama and not letting that fall be too bad. And for getting me here safely even though I drove like a bat out of you-know-where. But You know I'm not much of a nurse, Lord, so if You don't mind lending a hand while I take care of Mama the next few days, I sure will appreciate it."

Chapter 10

Mr. Clark was out on a job site, but Mr. Hasna was in when I got back to the office. I could tell he didn't like it much when I said I needed to take the rest of the week off to take care of my mama, but at least he didn't say no. Alison listened carefully all afternoon to my explanations of what would come across my desk to be handled while I was gone, and though she seemed a bit panicky to be left on her own, she told me she was going to put Mama on her church's prayer list. When I left at the end of the day, I felt a sense of relief that I had at least taken care of everything I could, and I wasn't leaving any messes for Alison to deal with.

Jolene at The Max wasn't nearly as understanding.

"What do you mean you can't work the rest of the week?"

she demanded, hands on her hips and her eyes glaring beneath bright blue eye shadow that went all the way up to her eyebrows. She stood in the middle of the server's alley, and we had to flatten ourselves against the wall to let a server with a loaded tray squeeze by.

"How am I supposed to cover your shifts? You're not giving me any advance warning, Mayla."

"You're getting almost as much advance warning as I got, Jolene. My mother broke her foot, it's not like she scheduled it to happen today. She needs me to take care of her."

"Can't you get someone else to do it? I mean, don't you have sisters and brothers? Doesn't she?"

I shook my head and tried to keep my temper in check. "There's only me and her."

"Well that was poor planning on someone's part, wasn't it?" Jolene snapped.

I rolled my eyes and was trying to think up an appropriately sarcastic response when Sylvia stepped from the bar into the alley.

"Oh, get off her back, Jolene. You know the rest of the servers will pitch in to pull her shifts for a few days. All you have to do is call them."

Jolene rounded on Sylvia. "Like I've got time to make all those calls."

Sylvia shrugged. "Okay, I'll call them if you're so busy. Quit making it sound like it's a big deal."

That silenced Jolene, who stood for a moment glaring back and forth from me to Sylvia. Then she muttered, "Fine," and stomped away.

I looked at Sylvia, feeling a little shy. We had not talked since our discussion about David and his wives, so I was surprised she had stuck up for me.

"Thanks. I appreciate it."

She shrugged again. "Not a biggie. So your mom broke her foot? Is she going to be okay?"

I nodded. "Yeah, I think she's fine. But when she comes home from the hospital tomorrow, the doctor said she can't put any weight on her foot at all, and all the bathrooms in that house are upstairs. So I'll just stay with her for a few days till she gets used to going up and down with the crutches. I was going to leave you a note at home."

Sylvia gave a single nod and started to turn away. Then she stopped and without looking up at my face said, "If there's anything I can do to help, let me know." Then she quickly walked away.

"Yeah, okay. Thanks," I told her retreating back.

I stood for a moment, looking after her. It had been brief, but it was the first friendly conversation we'd had in what seemed like months. I was surprised she had come to my defense with Jolene. I would have bet money that she would've rather seen me get fired from The Max and would have used it somehow to prove her point that being a Christian would bring me nothing but trouble. Maybe all those prayers Pastor Paul and I had been praying for Sylvia were starting to work.

Since I didn't have to go to the office in the morning, I slept later than usual and then got up and packed a suitcase with everything I would need to spend the next few days in Salliesburg. Before I left town, I stopped by St. Patrick's to let Alex know that I wouldn't be around for a few days. I also wanted to see if he was still speaking to me after I brought Lindsey to visit.

"Hey you," I said, walking into his room.

He looked even more tired than the day before, if that was possible, but at least he smiled when he saw me.

"Since you're not reaching for a bedpan to throw at me, can I assume I'm forgiven for contacting your family behind your back?"

"Well it was a dirty trick," he said, narrowing his eyes, "but since it turned out okay, yeah, I guess you're forgiven."

I heaved a dramatic sigh of relief and plopped down in the chair next to his bed. "So tell me all about it."

"I will, but first tell me why you're here in the morning instead of on your lunch hour. You didn't get fired, did you?"

"Ha! They wouldn't dare fire me," I joked. "I run the place. They wouldn't know what to do without me. But I have to go out of town for a couple of days."

I told him about Mama's accident, and I guess I must have lost my anxiety during the night because I found myself telling it like a joke, pleased when he chuckled at the appropriate parts, and laughing out loud with him when I got to the part about Mama's embarrassment at being done in by a box of maxi pads. Then he told me about his visit with Lindsey.

"It felt so good to sit back and listen to her talk about home," he said, smiling. "The last time I saw her she was only six, and now she's grown up into a young woman. And she's very strong, very determined."

"Yeah, I thought so, too. She reminded me a little of myself."

He thought about that. "Somewhat like you, I think. But a lot like my father. Whereas, I was always more like my mother, quiet and pliable, always doing what I was told."

"Pliable? You?" I shook my head. "If you were pliable, you would have become just what your father wanted you to be. Seems obvious to me that you stood up to him at least once."

Alex sighed. "Yeah, and of course that got me kicked out of the house. I guess there might be a little of him in me, but not much."

He paused, and I couldn't tell if he was catching his breath or considering what he was getting ready to say. Then he went on.

"Seeing Lindsey again has me thinking about my life. The worst parts have been when I felt alone. Even at home, before I came out, I was surrounded by family but I felt alone. It seems like all my life there's been someone who wanted me to be something I'm not, or do things I didn't want to do. There haven't been very many people who cared about me, who've been my friends just because they liked me. What I'd call real friends."

I started to interrupt him and tell him that I thought Lindsey was someone who cared about him no matter what, but he held up his hand and stopped me.

"What I've been thinking is that one of the few people who qualifies as a real friend is you. I just wanted you to know that, and I wanted to thank you for sneaking around behind my back and finding Lindsey. It meant more to me than I can say."

Tears prickled behind my eyes, and I tried to get a grip on them before they came gushing out and embarrassed both of us. I opened my mouth to tell him how much I liked Lindsey and how glad I was that it had turned out okay, but what came out instead surprised me so much that I nearly bit my tongue in half.

"You know, Alex, there is one Person who has loved you from the very beginning, and who has always loved you just the way you are. The reason I'm here is because He sent me to be your friend."

Where in the world had that come from? I really had not intended to say that! I was almost afraid to look at Alex, wondering if I had just alienated him beyond repair. Instead of being offended, though, he looked sad. He shook his head.

"It's too late for me, Mayla. I'm dying."

Encouraged, I leaned forward. "It's never too late, and especially if you're dying. The next life is a lot longer than this one, Alex. It lasts forever. And if you don't know Jesus, it will be a lot worse than this one ever was. All you have to do is pray that simple little prayer now, and—"

"And what? He'll heal me? It seems sort of hypocritical to become a Christian when I'm dying and not much use, don't you think? And if I suddenly recovered, would he make me promise to pretend I'm not gay anymore?"

His voice held a touch of anger, but mostly just sadness. I took a deep breath. I was way out of my league here, but I couldn't stop now. I had to plow ahead, even if I made a mess of things.

"Pretend for who?" I asked. "It's no good pretending anything for God, because He knows all there is to know about you. And I don't know if He would heal you or not. That doesn't seem to happen very often. I do know you'd feel better. Oh, not physically maybe, but inside, just like I did. It's hard to describe to someone who has never felt it, but it's a peace I can't explain. One thing I do know is that He loves you just as much now as He did the day you were born. He doesn't care if you live another day or a year or ten years—He just wants you to know how much He loves you, and He wants you to be with Him forever."

He sighed in frustration, his fists clenched. "I can't even get out of this bed to go home, much less go to church."

"Who said anything about church? You don't need a church. You don't even need a preacher. After all, this is a private thing between you and Jesus, and He's here all the time. You just have to pray a simple little prayer and ask Him to come into your heart and save you."

Was that right? I didn't know. After all, I had been in front of a whole congregation of people, and Pastor Paul had led me through the prayer. But it felt right. I couldn't imagine Jesus turning his back on Alex because he wasn't standing in front of a room full of people.

He looked at me for a long time, then slowly shook his head. "I don't know, Mayla. I'll think about it."

I stood. "You let me know if you need anything. The nurses have my cell phone number and they'll call me if you tell them to. When I come back in a few days I'm sure I'll have lots of stories to tell."

He smiled then. "I can't wait to hear them. Tell your mother I hope she feels better soon."

I walked out of Alex's room with one thought rolling around in my head. *Lord, that was You talking in there, not me. So keep working on him, please, because that man needs You more than anyone I ever knew. And quick.*

I made an important discovery while taking care of Mama over the next few days. I will never be a nurse. I think I'm a pretty good visitor to sick people like Alex, and I do okay help-ing out here and there if someone needs an errand run while they recover. But after days of trying to take care of my mama, whom I love most in the world next to Jesus, I learned what it means to have the "gift of nursing." It's not necessarily the gift of knowing how to do things other people don't—after all, you can learn that stuff in school. The gift is that those people actually like it; it's a gift of being happy and cheerful while you're doing it. That's the piece I don't have.

Part of the problem was Mama, who is maybe the most stubborn sick person in the world. She wants things done her way, and she does not trust anyone else to do it her way. Take cooking, for instance. Most people would be grateful for someone coming in to cook their meals for them. Mama kept following me around, hobbling on the crutches she was only supposed to use to go to the bathroom, salting the chicken noodle soup behind my back or adding more mayonnaise to the bologna sandwiches. It drove me nuts how she refused to stay on the couch and watch television or read a book like she was supposed to.

I couldn't clean a room to suit her, either. That, at least, had not changed from when I lived at home. I have already established that I am not the neatest person in the world, but most of that is by choice. Mama raised me knowing how to clean a house, but I sure didn't like it and I didn't do it willingly. We had some memorable battles over my room when I was a kid.

This time, instead of yelling at me, she followed me around and straightened pillows or rearranged the forty gazillion Precious Moments figurines after I had moved them to dust the tables they sat on. It wasn't so bad making the beds and cleaning the bathroom, because she couldn't yet manage the stairs without my help. But I would come back downstairs to find everything . . . neater. And there she would be, sitting on the sofa with her cast propped up on its pile of pillows, innocently sipping tea and reading a book like she had never moved.

The worst part was the boredom. Mama wasn't really sick after all; she just couldn't get around very well. I helped her get cleaned up in the morning as best we could manage without getting the cast wet, then I maneuvered her down the stairs and made breakfast. Cooking isn't one of my gifts, either, so breakfast was cold cereal with bananas. I can slice a mean banana. Then I'd get Mama settled on the couch and go upstairs to make the beds and straighten up the bedrooms. After that, it was a long time till lunch, and even longer till supper, and Mama nearly drove me nuts wanting to read me jokes from *Reader's Digest*. I felt like I had to sit in the room and listen to her. In the afternoon, she spent several hours on her computer, answering e-mails from all over the world and sitting in on her favorite Christian chat room while I wandered around the house looking for something to do. I mean, there's only so many times you can dust before you start rubbing the finish off the furniture.

Thank goodness for the prayer chain. By the end of the second day, the entire church had been alerted to Mama's accident and the visitors started coming that afternoon. They usually showed up in pairs, and they always came bearing the universally acknowledged symbol of wishes for speedy recovery—the casserole. So not only did they keep us entertained, but we ate pretty well too. Microwaving casseroles is one of my most successful domestic skills, second only to slicing bananas.

On Friday morning, I woke to the sound of a lawn mower, its buzzing drone muffled through the windows and curtains and the fluffy foam pillow covering my head. Reaching up to move one corner of the pillow, I peeked out from my cocoon to squint at the red digital numbers on the alarm clock. 7:36.

"Who the heck is mowing their grass at this ungodly hour of the morning?" I grumbled to myself.

Mama must have been listening for sounds coming from my room, because she instantly called, "Mayla, are you up?"

Stifling a groan, I whipped the pillow off of my head.

"Yeah, I'm up," I shouted back. "Who could sleep through that racket? Which one of your crazy neighbors mows their grass at the crack of dawn, anyway?"

I heard the floorboards creak and the sound of Mama's bedroom slipper sliding across the hallway floor. As I sat up in bed, she appeared in my doorway, propped expertly between two crutches, her injured foot hovering six inches off the floor.

"It's not one of my crazy neighbors. It's Mr. Holmes from the church. He's mowin' my grass for me, bless his heart."

"Mr. Holmes?" I threw back the comforter and slipped my feet into the fuzzy slippers I kept at Mama's house. "You're kidding."

"Uh-uh, he showed up about fifteen minutes ago. I heard his truck pull in the driveway, and a'course I woulda gone down and offered him coffee, but—"

She shook a crutch in my direction with a wry twist of her lips.

Crossing to my bedroom window, I pulled aside the white curtain and peered outside. Sure enough, there was Mr. Holmes, both hands on the bar of an ancient-looking power mower, making his way slowly across the front yard and leaving a neatly trimmed swath behind him. I took a deep breath and smelled the tangy sweet scent of freshly cut grass.

Keeping my gaze fixed on the old man's slowly moving figure, I spoke to Mama, who had hobbled over to the window to stand beside me.

"What in the world is he doing?"

"I'm guessin' he heard about my accident from someone at the church, and he came to do a good deed."

"That old grouch?" I snorted. "Hard to believe."

Mama shook her head as we watched Mr. Holmes navigate a turn at the corner of the yard. "He's a nice man, once you get past the gruff. Lonely, though. Lost his wife years ago. They say she was a pistol, always laughin' and pullin' pranks. Opposites attract, I guess."

"No kids?" I asked.

"None that I ever heard about."

We stood for another moment while he passed the length of the front yard again and disappeared around the far side of the house. Mama turned on her crutches.

"C'mon and help me down them stairs so I can get me some coffee. What're you fixin' for breakfast?"

"Corn flakes," I replied. "With sliced bananas."

She chuckled. "What else?"

The hum of the lawn mower stopped as we finished our cereal. I settled Mama on the couch and reluctantly went to the front door. Through the window, I saw Mr. Holmes slamming shut the tailgate of his beat-up old pickup truck, the mower stored in the bed. Apparently he planned to leave without saying a word to Mama and me.

I stepped out onto the porch as he walked around the driver's side. He paused when he caught sight of me.

"Uh, hi," I said, trotting down the stairs and toward the truck. "Thanks for mowing the grass. That was nice of you."

He shrugged and ducked his head, avoiding my gaze.

"Would you like to come in and have a cup of coffee, or maybe some iced tea? Mama would like to thank you in person, but she can't really manage to come outside just yet."

Shaking his head, he answered in his gravelly voice, his eyes fixed on something inside the truck's cab. "Gotta git home. She okay, your mama?"

"She's going to be fine. She just needs to rest and let her foot heal."

He nodded and opened the cab door. "She needs anything, you let me know and I'll be 'round directly."

"I will, Mr. Holmes. And thanks again."

I retreated to the porch and stood watching as he backed out of the driveway. Imagine that old grouch, coming to mow Mama's grass! He seemed embarrassed to be caught in the act of doing a good deed. Go figure. I shook my head, watching him shift the truck out of reverse. Just as he went past the porch, he looked directly at me. Giving a curt nod, he turned his head and drove slowly away.

An hour later the phone rang.

"Hello?"

"Hi, Mayla. Pastor Paul. How's the recovery going?"

"Okay," I told him. "She's getting around in the cast pretty well. Going up the stairs is a snap if she just remembers to take it slow, but coming down is still a challenge. The hard part is keeping her off her feet like the doctor said."

I glared at Mama and she stuck out her tongue, then went back to her book.

"Well, tell her she's in my prayers. Actually, I was calling to ask a favor, but I don't want you to feel like you have to do it if you're too busy. I know taking care of Angela comes first."

I snorted. "She's a handful all right, but I find I have some free time. What do you need?"

"Sharon is out of town this week visiting her sister in Florida, and she had made arrangements with Lucille Miller to do the church bulletin. But Lucille called me yesterday, and she's got the flu or something so she can't do it either. I can use a computer well enough to check my e-mail and type my sermon notes, but I don't have the slightest idea how to do formatting and all that. Do you?"

"I sure do," I told him. "I use a computer all day long at work."

"Do you think you could figure out how to do the bulletin? It will need to be done pretty quickly."

It sounded like my kind of project, and just what I needed to keep me busy. "Sure. Want me to come over to the church and you can show me what you have?"

He paused, and when he answered he sounded embarrassed. "Uh, I don't think that would be a good idea with Sharon out of town. It wouldn't look right."

I felt a flash of heat in my face, but I didn't take the time to wonder whether it was from anger or embarrassment, or to keep it out of my voice. "And why not?"

He cleared his throat. "It's not a reflection on you, Mayla. It's just that I'm a single man, and a preacher, and I have to be aware of appearances. Some people might think it's inappropriate for me to be alone with a young woman in the church."

"Well that's just ridiculous," I snapped.

Even as I said it, I knew he was right. What a tough life he must have, living in a small town like Salliesburg and trying to make sure he didn't do anything that would set the gossip lines buzzing. I had never worried about things like that. In fact, I always got a certain enjoyment out of creating opportunities for gossip.

"Uh, anyway, doesn't Angela have a computer you can use? I get e-mails from her, so I assumed she did."

"Yes, she has one upstairs. She's got a printer, too."

"If you could get this done it would be a big help." He sounded relieved. "I'll stop by this afternoon and bring all the information, and we'll figure it out."

"Okay, I'll see you then."

✝

Pastor Paul showed up carrying a pair of bulging manila envelopes just as the five o'clock news came on. A light breeze had ruffled his dark hair, and he wore jeans and a white golf shirt open at the neck. I realized with a start that he didn't look nearly as preacher-like without his suit and tie, but more like a regular guy.

"Uh, hi," I said, trying not to show how flustered I suddenly felt. "Come on in."

I stood back to let him through the door as Mama called from the living room, "Hi there, Pastor."

"Hello, Angela." I caught a faint whiff of his spicy aftershave as he walked past me and into the living room to take Mama's hand and give it a squeeze. "How are you feeling?"

"Absolutely fine. Not a thing wrong with me, no matter what they say," she told him, glancing defiantly at me. "It doesn't even hurt."

"Well give God thanks for that," he told her, "and follow the doctor's orders so it stays that way."

I smirked at her and she rolled her eyes.

"Can't help but follow the doctor's orders with the warden here standin' guard over every little thing I do."

He laughed. "Well keep in mind what it says in Jeremiah 31: 'There is hope for your future,' declares the Lord. 'Your children will return to their own land.'"

I laughed out loud.

"Leave it to a preacher to have a Bible verse handy for every situation," Mama said, chuckling.

"Naturally." He held the envelopes out toward me. "I think I got everything you'll need. I even brought last week's bulletin to use as a sample."

"That's great," I said, taking it from him. "Thanks."

I didn't move, and he stood looking at me expectantly. "Uh, I thought maybe we could go over it, you know, just to see if you have any questions."

Mama piped in, "Why don't you go on into the kitchen so you can spread it all out on the table, Mayla. And maybe Pastor Paul would like a Diet Coke."

He smiled. "That sounds good."

I didn't want to invite him into the kitchen for a Diet Coke. I could tell this man my most personal thoughts on the telephone and it felt like the most natural thing in the world. And I could listen to him preach from the pulpit for hours and hang on every word that came out of his mouth. But standing here in front of me, wearing clothes that any old guy might wear, he just seemed too normal. Not like a preacher at all. With our phone conversation burning embarrassingly in the front of my mind, I felt funny being alone with him, even with Mama in the next room.

I couldn't very well say that, so I turned around abruptly and went into the kitchen. He followed and emptied the contents of the envelopes onto the table as I filled two glasses with ice and soda. When I joined him, he had everything laid out neatly.

"Here's your model," he said, pointing toward last week's bulletin. "It pretty much follows the same format every week. I realized on the way over that I can e-mail you last week's file so you can just copy the format."

I shrugged. "It's not necessary. This isn't hard to do."

"Okay, if you're sure. Besides the order of service there's a couple of inserts we need to do as well. Back at the church office I've got some yellow paper because Ted wanted the choir insert printed on yellow. The rest of the announcements can just go on regular white paper. Here's a few sample blank bulletins to work with."

He pointed to several sheets of paper preprinted on one side with a colorful photo of an arrangement of daisies on a polished wooden altar, an illuminated cross in the background.

"How many copies do you need?"

"A hundred, but if you just get me one good master I can run the rest of them through the copier at the church office. That's how we usually do it."

While I went through the handwritten notes to make sure I could read them, he leaned back easily in the kitchen chair, sipping his Coke and rocking on two legs with the balance of an athlete. I did my best to concentrate on the papers and ignore him, but it was hard with him watching me read.

"You seem on edge," he said suddenly. "Is something wrong?"

I shook my head guiltily. "No, of course not. Everything's fine."

He lowered his voice. "I wondered if maybe taking care of her," he inclined his head toward the living room, "was rougher than you expected."

"It isn't easy," I admitted. "She's stubborn as a mule and twice as ornery, but I hold my own."

He laughed quietly. "I'll bet you do. Hey, I wanted to ask how it's going with Sylvia."

I picked up my Coke. "Oh, you're not going to believe this." I told him about our conversation at The Max. "I couldn't believe she actually stood up for me, and even volunteered to find people to fill my shifts. That's the first nice thing she's done for me since I was baptized."

He rocked back and forth on the chair, nodding. "Keep praying for her. Something tells me she's got a lot of pain she's trying to deal with. It sounds like you're starting to get through to her. And what about Alex? What's the latest on his family?"

"Gosh, I haven't told you about Lindsey!"

"Who's Lindsey?"

I brought him up to date on Alex's sister, ending with our most recent conversation. While I talked, all the awkwardness went away—simply evaporated—and before I knew it I wasn't talking to a good-looking guy anymore. He was once again just Pastor Paul. I finished by saying, "I wish he would let you visit so you could tell him all the things he needs to know. I fumble around and say the wrong thing most of the time."

Pastor Paul shook his head. "I think you did just fine. I would only make him uncomfortable because I'm a stranger and a preacher. You've given him what he needed, which was a friend and an introduction to Jesus. Now it's up to him."

"Mayla," shouted Mama from the living room. "Have you asked the preacher to stay to supper?"

"Not yet," I shouted back, then grinned at him. "We're having Mrs. Caldwell's chicken-and-rice casserole, Mrs. Warren's broccoli casserole, and Mrs. Pritchard's potato salad. And for dessert, Gladys Howard made an apple pie."

He licked his lips appreciatively. "Sounds better than the peanut butter sandwich that's waiting for me at home. I'd love to stay, if you're sure you have enough."

"Believe me," I told him as I stood, "we have plenty. And when we finish these, I'm sure someone else will come visiting with more. If you don't mind putting this stuff away, I'll start heating things up."

I threw myself into that bulletin. Finally, I had something to do! Mama grumbled about missing out on her regular chat room conversation, but after a while she got interested in a television show and left me alone. By ten o'clock, I had everything typed, formatted, and the master copy printed. I shut down the computer, gave it a satisfied pat, and went downstairs to help Mama get ready for bed.

The next morning, I called Pastor Paul and told him I had the masters ready. He said he was working on his sermon, but he came right over. Instead of coming inside, he stood on the front porch and glanced through my work. I could tell he was in a hurry to get back to the church and finish his sermon.

"Everything looks great, Mayla," he told me, putting the pages carefully back into the envelope. "I can't thank you enough. A couple of the youth are going to come by the church tonight to make the copies and assemble them."

Relieved, I realized that the awkwardness from the day before had disappeared. Once again he was just my pastor. As I stood on the porch and watched his Escort back out of Mama's driveway, I realized how much I had enjoyed the little bulletin project. It had provided a brief but much needed distraction from my nursing duties.

Chapter 11

Somewhere in Proverbs it says that people find rewards in the work of their hands. I know that's true, but I have to say I felt much more rewarded by my work at the construction office than I did taking care of my mama. When I walked through the office door the next Monday morning, I was practically rejoicing.

Mama had finally learned to navigate the stairs with the crutches. I had awakened Sunday morning to the aroma of bacon sizzling downstairs, and I breathed a heartfelt, "Thank you, Lord!" The first meal I hadn't cooked—or reheated—in a week tasted especially good because Mama had managed it alone, and I knew my time of service had finally come to an end. I could "return to my own land," as Pastor Paul had said.

Alison was overjoyed to have me back.

"You can't imagine how glad I am to see you," she told me as she walked through the door behind me. "Fields Lumber says they haven't been paid and they're refusing to deliver our orders. We had a walk-off on the Sanford Avenue job on Thursday, and Mr. Clark was there all day Thursday and Friday trying to calm things down. And then APS shorted us twenty paychecks in the package on Friday!"

She collapsed into her chair. "I was on the phone for hours trying to get the right net pay amounts from APS so I could write manual checks. The guys were all standing in here, listening to every word, and they weren't smiling."

I could imagine. Our payroll service was normally pretty good, but this wasn't the first time they had missed a stack of checks. I had worked under the oppressing glare of a crowd of angry construction workers several times, and it wasn't fun. I could handle the heat, but Alison tended to collapse into a flustered heap at the first cross word.

"But you got it done!" I congratulated her. "Good job. And don't worry about Fields Lumber. I'll talk to Shawn in invoicing over there and figure out what the problem is."

She sat back in her chair with a sigh of relief.

"I'm so glad you're back, Mayla. How's your mother?"

"Stubborn," I told her, rolling my eyes. "And better, thanks."

I settled in at my desk and dove into the work, thankful for the blessing of a busy job.

Half an hour before quitting time, my cell phone rang.

"Hello?"

"Miss Strong? This is Gail Lewis at St. Patrick's."

My stomach gave a little flutter. "Is Alex okay?"

"Oh, yes. I'm calling because he is being released tomorrow."

"Released? He must have gotten better pretty quick, then." I propped the cell phone on my shoulder so I could use both hands to file the day's paperwork while I talked. "Last time I saw him he didn't look like he was even close to being released."

There was a pause. "Well, to be honest, he's not any better." Her voice was quiet and deliberate. "He has asked to be released. He says he's tired of hospitals and he wants to go home. He's insistent, and his doctor is honoring his wishes."

During the silence that followed, my mind tried to reject the message she was delivering. Alex was not better, and his doctor had agreed to send him home. That could only mean one thing.

"He's going home to die?" I asked, unsurprised to hear my voice quiver.

"I'm afraid so. I'm calling because he told me he's planning to take a taxi home. I just thought it would be better if he had someone he knows to pick him up and drive him."

I sat there struggling with my thoughts. I couldn't take off work again, not so soon after being gone the previous week. While I was taking care of Mama, Stuart had called to tell me that Stephen had moved out. The thought of Alex being dropped off by an uncaring taxi driver and having to carry his stuff upstairs to his empty apartment was more than I could bear. I couldn't let that happen.

"Is there any way you can keep him there until around noon?" I asked.

"I can arrange that," she told me, relief apparent in her voice. "The doctor won't show up until nine or ten, and then the release paperwork has to be done. I'll make sure it's not ready until you get here."

"Okay, I'll be there at noon."

I punched the End button and dialed Stuart.

"Hey, it's Mayla. Can you get the key to Alex's apartment from Stephen? I need to go over there tonight. Alex is coming home tomorrow."

"You gotta be kidding! I was at the hospital a couple of days ago and he looked . . . oh." Stuart was quiet a moment. "Okay, I'll see what I can do."

"Thanks. If you want to go with me, I could use the company. I want to take inventory, make sure he has food and all that."

"I've got a thing tonight, but I'll run by the grocery store first and whip up a batch of chicken soup."

"Great, Stuart. Later."

I sighed as I disconnected the call. *Lord,* I thought, *can't You do something for Alex?*

I heard His voice then, quiet and distinctively firm in my mind. He said, *I am.* And I knew He meant He was sending me.

I stayed late at work and got all the filing done, and when I got home another surprise awaited me.

Sylvia was curled up on the couch watching a *Home Improvement* rerun.

"I'll go with you," she volunteered when I told her about my plans for the evening.

Trying not to show how her offer had stunned me, I said, "Great. Let me get changed first and then we'll go."

I pulled on some jeans and a tee shirt and slipped on my tennis shoes. After a moment's hesitation, I picked up my Bible and shook out the little slips of paper I used to mark passages I wanted to remember. I liked that Bible; it had some sentimental value because it had been a baptism gift from Pastor Paul.

And the pages were marked up, because I liked to underline verses I thought were important. But I could get another Bible. I stuffed it in a grocery sack so I wouldn't antagonize Sylvia.

She had been busy while I changed. She had her own bag, full of cleaning stuff, sitting by the door. She came out of the kitchen carrying a broom and a mop.

"We don't know what shape Stephen left it in," she told me by way of explanation. "I'm sure it needs a *thorough* cleaning."

I noted her emphasis and grinned. The implication that I couldn't manage a thorough cleaning was not lost on me.

"I'm sure Alex will appreciate it."

While Sylvia loaded her supplies in the car, I ran upstairs and pounded on Stuart's door. He opened it with a flourish.

"I just finished," he announced, then fished in his pocket and thrust a key into my hand. "Don't even ask me what a jerk Stephen was when I picked it up. He's a real fiend. Grab a sack."

He pointed to five or six full plastic grocery sacks sitting on the dinette table.

"Holy cow, Stuart! You went overboard."

"Nah, not really. I got stuff that will be easy for him to fix, just heat-and-eat things mostly. And milk and cheese and bread. If there is any of that left in the apartment, it won't be good. Oh, and look at this!" He opened one of the bags. "I got some of those disposable plastic thingies and fixed up individual servings of my homemade chicken soup. All he has to do is put it in the microwave and he has a home-cooked meal."

I grinned. "You're awesome. You really are."

Stuart ran a hand through his spiky blondish hair. "Nah, this is nothing. I wish I could get out of this thing tonight and help you, but I just can't. Tell Alex I'll come by tomorrow night to make sure he's settled in okay."

I hugged him and kissed his cheek. "Will do."

Alex lived in an apartment complex on the other side of town, and the ride over there was one of the most uncomfortable I've ever had. After the initial questions about Mama's accident and recovery, Sylvia made no attempt at conversation but sat silently in the passenger seat, staring out the window. It was an awkward silence, one I wanted to fill with the easy chatter we used to enjoy back before I became a Christian. I couldn't think of a thing to say that wouldn't set her off. It felt like walking on a tightrope; I knew if I took one wrong step I would fall. It made me sad, because I missed our friendship and I hated the tension that was always between us now.

Sylvia was right. Stephen had left the apartment a complete wreck. Dishes had been piled on the kitchen counters with food dried into cement all over them. He hadn't bothered to clean the floors under the furniture he had moved, nor did it look like he had cleaned beneath them in months. I wrinkled my nose at an unpleasant smell, probably coming from the decaying food in the kitchen.

The place looked sad and half empty. The living room contained a couch with a table in front of it and a television sitting on the floor, a crushed outline in the carpet to show where the entertainment center had been. One bedroom had only odds and ends in it, a bookcase and a lamp on the floor in one corner, but the other bedroom was relatively intact. The single bathroom definitely needed a good scrubbing all over.

After a brief, silent walk-through, Sylvia took charge.

"Okay, first let's bring the stuff up from the car, and then you strip the sheets off the bed," she ordered. "Thank goodness he has a washer and dryer so we don't have to mess with going to a Laundromat. Walk around and grab anything cloth you see and get a load of wash going. I'll start in the kitchen."

I did as directed. It's easier to clean when someone's telling you what to do. I also discovered that cleaning Alex's apartment gave me a feeling of satisfaction I had never felt before. I guess I was being rewarded by the work of my hands.

While we worked, the awkward silence from the car was replaced by our exclamations of dismay over the dirt we scrubbed away and our mutual disgust for Stephen. Had he walked through the door that evening, either of us would have cheerfully held his head in the toilet while the other flushed. It gave us a common goal, and when we left at almost eleven o'clock, the atmosphere between us was easier than it had been in weeks. Sylvia didn't even comment when I placed my Bible on the nightstand beside Alex's freshly made bed.

On the way home, Sylvia became quiet again. It wasn't the awkwardness I had felt before, just the silence of tiredness that comes after you've done something nice for a friend. She only spoke once, and she didn't look at me when she did.

"I think it's really great what you've done for Alex. You've been a real Christian."

I wanted to tell her that although I may have started visiting Alex because it was the Christian thing to do, I had come to care for him. I had become his friend, and anything I did for him was for the sake of friendship. I think that's how God works in us—at first we act out of obedience, and then He changes us from the inside. But my throat tightened when I realized that for the first time she had said the word without anger or sarcasm.

I found that all I could say was, "Thanks."

Chapter 12

On Tuesday morning at ten, my cell phone rang. I was writing out the check to Fields Lumber for the invoice we hadn't received, and I planned to drop it by their office on my way to the hospital.

"Hello?"

"Miss Strong?"

I knew immediately that something was terribly wrong. Nurse Gail's voice sounded different from the day before, tighter, more controlled. I put down my pen and turned my chair so I faced the wall, my back to the desk where Alison sat typing a letter on her computer.

"What is it?"

As I asked the question, I realized she didn't need to answer. I already knew.

"He's gone, Mayla," she said softly. "He died at 7:54 this morning. I'm so sorry."

My cheeks felt suddenly cold and clammy, as if all the blood had run out of them. I tried to speak, but found I couldn't get a sound past the tightness in my throat.

Gail continued, "He had a heart attack. It's not uncommon, really. His body was in such a weakened state that it couldn't go on." She paused. "Thank goodness I got a phone number from his sister last week. I've called his parents, and his father said they would make the final arrangements. He asked for a list of crematories to contact, and I put them in touch with the hospital social worker."

She stopped again, and I still said nothing. I couldn't. My mind was trying to grasp the fact that Alex was dead. We had cleaned his apartment, stocked his refrigerator, Stuart had made soup! How could he be dead?

"Mayla? Are you still there?"

I cleared my throat and managed a shaky yes.

She went on in a softer voice. "I was with him at the end, Mayla. He was okay. And he was thinking of you. That's what I called to tell you, because he gave me a message for you. He said, 'Tell Mayla "thanks." She was right.'"

I swallowed, hard. "I was right? About what?"

"I don't know. Maybe he meant you were right to call his sister. I do know he seemed calm. Almost happy. I know how much he appreciated your friendship."

There was another long pause while I lost a struggle to keep the tears from rolling down my cheeks. I took a deep, ragged breath, aware that behind me Alison had stopped typing.

"Listen, I've got to go," Gail told me. "I wanted to give you that message, and I wanted to stop you before you got over here at noon. Are you going to be okay?"

"Yeah, sure," I whispered. Whispers were safer. You couldn't hear the tears in a whisper. "I'll be fine. Thanks for calling."

I punched the End button and sat still for a moment, remembering Alex as he had been the last time I saw him. He had been weak, but happier because of Lindsey's visit. I had told him how to accept Jesus as his personal Savior and Lord. Had he done it? Had he? Was that what he meant by, "She was right"? Or had he simply meant, as Gail suggested, that I had been right to contact his family?

Lord, what does it mean? I cried silently. Then I realized I wasn't crying silently. I was crying for real with deep, shuddering sobs. Alison was beside me in a moment, her hands on my shoulders.

"What's wrong?" she whispered as she hugged me. "What happened?"

I shook my head, struggling to get control of myself. "A friend just died."

Her grip tightened. "Oh, Mayla, I'm so sorry."

I pulled away from her, tears still streaming, and reached for my purse. "I've got to get out of here for a while. I'm taking an early lunch, okay?"

"Sure, honey, just go. Don't come back today. I can handle things here. Take as long as you need."

I tried to smile my gratitude, but I'm sure it looked more like a grimace. I practically ran out the door, aware that she stood beside my chair watching me, her brow creased with worry.

I ran for my car and started it mindlessly. Then I drove. I didn't consciously head for Salliesburg, but that's where I found myself going. My mind was busy feeling the pain, remembering Alex lying weak and pale in bed, imagining Lindsey's grief when she learned of her brother's death.

All the while, I knew I should pray, but I didn't. God hadn't answered my prayers to save Alex, had He? He hadn't healed Alex. Instead He had sent me into that hospital room on purpose, had made me befriend Alex knowing all along that this would happen, that I would feel this pain. Why? Why?

My questions were not asked of God. They were thrown angrily and sorrowfully into the void that my suffering was creating between Him and me. Instead of turning to Him for comfort, I writhed alone with my grief.

As I pulled into the church parking lot, I saw three other cars—Pastor Paul's in the "Reserved for Pastor" parking space, one I didn't recognize, and Mr. Holmes's pickup. I whipped my own car into the first empty space and proceeded briskly to the front door, not stopping to calm myself down. I stomped through the sanctuary toward the office, bursting through the door without knocking.

Sharon, the church secretary, back from vacation, looked up with a start and then smiled. "Mayla! It's good to see—" She caught sight of my face. "What's wrong?"

I shook my head, skirting her desk and barging into the preacher's office.

Pastor Paul sat behind a desk covered with opened books and his big black Bible, handwritten notes littering the surface. He looked up, surprised, and brightened when he saw me. Then he noticed my face. I hadn't bothered to dry my cheeks, and my eyes felt puffy from crying. He stood, coming around the desk toward me.

"What is it? What's happened? Is Angela—"

"She's fine," I said quickly. "It's Alex. He's—" I gulped back a sob. "He's dead."

Hot tears gushed in my eyes and Pastor Paul's face creased with sorrow.

"Oh, Mayla, I'm so sorry. How? When?"

"This morning," I sobbed. "Heart attack. He was supposed to go home today. I was going to take him. Sylvia and I cleaned his apartment. We washed the sheets."

I broke then and couldn't say another word. Waves of tears poured down my cheeks and I felt my knees buckle. Pastor Paul steadied me with a firm hand on my shoulder and led me to a chair near his desk. He called for Sharon, who bustled through the open doorway with a box of tissues. Pastor Paul knelt beside me, a comforting hand on my arm, as I cried with a fierceness that surprised me. I couldn't remember ever totally losing it like this, even when my father died.

I don't know how long it lasted, but eventually it became awkward to sit there with the preacher kneeling beside me and his secretary handing me a new tissue whenever the last one became too damp to use. I forced myself to stop, though tears continued to seep from my eyes. Sharon slipped discreetly back to her office, leaving the door cracked open.

"That's better," said Pastor Paul when my shuddering breath had calmed.

He pulled a chair beside mine and sat facing me.

"Now, can you tell me about it?"

I did, concluding with Alex's message to me. He listened, nodding to encourage me when I faltered.

"I don't know what that message meant either, Mayla, and we will probably never know this side of heaven. But I think the Lord wouldn't mind if we make an assumption that Alex accepted Him at the end."

I shook my head. "I can't make an assumption like that. What if it's wrong?"

Pastor Paul shrugged. "What if it is?"

Irritation rose up in me and I jerked out of the chair, striding across the room. "Because I want the truth, that's what. I want to know if my friendship with Alex did any good or if it was for nothing!"

His gaze pierced mine. "How could friendship ever be for nothing?"

Ashamed, I looked away. "You're right. Alex appreciated my friendship, and I appreciated his, too."

"Of course you did. I firmly believe that God sent you into Alex's life for a reason, and I think it was to introduce him to Jesus. But even if he decided not to accept the Lord's invitation, that doesn't invalidate anything you did. God weighs the motives in our hearts, and He rewards us accordingly."

"Ha! Some reward," I almost spat. The anger that flared into my voice surprised me, and from his face I could tell it surprised Pastor Paul, too. I hadn't been this angry for months, not since I had become a believer. I plowed ahead, caught up in a fit of rage. "God knew what was going to happen, but He let me go in there last night and clean that apartment. And I got other people involved, too, Stuart and Sylvia. And for what? Nothing. Alex didn't even know we did it."

His voice remained calm, a stark difference from mine. "I think he does. But even if he didn't know before he died, so what? Stuart knows. Sylvia knows. Mayla, kindness is a fruit of the Holy Spirit. It's part of what happens in us when we invite Him into our lives. We aren't kind so that people will notice, we're kind because God is kind and we reflect His character."

I shouted then, "It hurts to be kind! It hurts a lot! Why does God want to hurt people?"

We stared at each other in the silence that followed, me shocked that I had just yelled at the preacher, and Pastor Paul watching me with his face impassive. Outside the office, there was a brief pause in the tapping on Sharon's keyboard. When

Pastor Paul finally spoke, his voice held so much gentleness that fresh tears sprang to my eyes.

"He doesn't want to hurt you, Mayla. He loves you. He knows the pain you're feeling. Why do you think he's called the Man of Sorrows?"

"Then why didn't He save Alex?" I whispered, sniffling.

He smiled. "I think He did."

Sylvia put things into a different perspective when I got home that afternoon. She was shocked to hear of Alex's death, but when I told her how angry I was that all our work the night before had been for nothing, she shrugged.

"Maybe not," she told me. "I mean, if you look at the practical aspect, someone had to do it after he died anyway. At least now his family won't have to walk into the mess we found."

I spared an unkind thought for Alex Markham Sr. "I'm not sure his father will appreciate the gesture."

"You're probably right, but he would certainly think worse of Alex if he saw that mess," she pointed out. "Now maybe he'll have at least one nice thought of his son, even if it's only that he was clean. So look at it like one final favor to Alex. Besides, you know what they say. No act of kindness goes unrewarded."

Pastor Paul could have uttered that same thought. But before I could comment on it, she turned away and headed down the hall toward her room to get ready for work.

When I got to the office the next morning, Alison was already there, and I found a sympathy card propped up on my keyboard. She waved off my apologies for leaving her stranded so soon after being off for a week.

"You were really upset," she said. "You wouldn't have been able to work anyway. Did you go see your mama?"

I shook my head. "I went to see my pastor."

Smiling, she gave my shoulder a gentle pat. "That was better anyway. We need spiritual counseling when we're in grief."

I thought then how Alison had changed from the arrogant prima donna she used to be. Though she looked and dressed exactly the same, she had been changed on the inside and it showed. Just like me.

But was I really changed? If I was so different, then why was I reacting so badly to Alex's death? I had spent a long night thinking about it, and if I was honest with myself I knew it wasn't only grief I felt. It was personal failure. I had been given an important task and I had failed at it. And I was angry with God for giving me the task to begin with. He knew what would happen, and I felt like He had set me up for failure and disappointment.

In the darkness of my bedroom and the quiet of the early morning, I had seen how unchristian my feelings were, and I wept new tears. I so wanted to be different than I was before, to be loving and kind just for the sake of being loving and kind. My friendship with Alex had been real, I knew that. But all along I had been secretly selfish, secretly wanting people like Pastor Paul and Mama to notice how Christlike I was acting. And I had so wanted Alex to accept Jesus. For his own sake, yes. But also so I could brag to Pastor Paul about it, so he would know that it was me who had done it. It had been a way of getting attention, just like piercing my labret.

I should have prayed then, should have confessed my shameful conceit to my Father in heaven. But the anger was still there, and I didn't feel like God and I were on speaking terms at the moment. The void I had created still gaped between us, raw and hurting like an open wound. I knew God was on the other side of that void, waiting for me to talk to Him, wanting to forgive me, but I just couldn't make myself pray.

At lunchtime, I went to Alex's apartment. I still had his key, and I thought I would let myself in, get my Bible and leave the key on the kitchen counter. When I opened the door I found I wasn't alone.

"Mayla!"

Lindsey Markham came running across the room and flung herself into my arms, sobbing. I stood frozen in one place, surprised, then put my arms around her and patted her back. A moment later, she got herself under control and pulled awkwardly away.

"I can't believe he's dead!"

"I know," I told her. "It happened so quick. He was supposed to come home today."

"Yeah, that's what the hospital told Daddy when they called. A heart attack. I still can't believe it."

She shook her head, her dark ponytail whipping around behind her. Then I saw that we were not alone; a woman stood uncertainly in the center of the nearly empty living room, watching us.

The one word that accurately described Alex's mother was timid. She looked like an older, paler version of both Alex and Lindsey, but without Lindsey's vitality or Alex's ready smile. Her dark hair was thinner than her daughter's, streaked with gray and hanging limply from a part in the center of her head. She was very thin, almost frail, and wore an unflattering gray sweater over baggy black slacks. The skin on her face was blotchy as if she had been crying recently, and I saw no sign of makeup. She didn't look like a woman who normally wore makeup.

I took a step toward her, my hand outstretched. "Mrs. Markham, I'm Mayla Strong, a friend of Alex's. I can't tell you how sorry I am."

Her gaze dropped to my labret stud, but her expression remained the same. She clasped my hand briefly in a grip as limp as her hair.

"My daughter has told me about you, Miss Strong."

I gave Lindsey a quick glance, wondering if I was going to get in trouble for helping her ditch school to visit her brother.

"It's okay," Lindsey said. "Mom understands, and we're both really glad I got to see Alex before . . . before the end."

I glanced at Mrs. Markham. How could a mother turn her back on her own son, even when she knew he was dying? I must not have succeeded in keeping my face impassive, because her gaze dropped away from mine.

"My husband doesn't know about Lindsey's visit," she said, haltingly. "He would be very upset if he did. He wouldn't allow any of us to contact Alex. He felt it was best if we kept our distance. He has a very important job in a bank, you see, and a reputation to think of."

I turned away then, certain that I could not keep the disgust off of my face. What kind of mother would allow a man, any man, to keep her away from her own son for the sake of his reputation? I walked quickly into the kitchen.

"I just came because I have a key to the apartment and I wanted to leave it. And also to pick up something of mine."

Lindsey and Mrs. Markham both followed me.

"We came to get Alex's personal stuff, papers and things like that," Lindsey told me while her mother stood silently in a corner, carefully looking anywhere but at me. "Daddy's at the funeral home now, making the arrangements. We're going to have a private ceremony down in Pikeville, just for family."

I nodded and fished in my purse for the key.

Mrs. Markham said, "The apartment certainly is clean. Someone must have cleaned it for him to come home today."

They both looked at me expectantly, but I shrugged. "Alex had lots of friends."

Lindsey said, "We're going to give the furniture and stuff to charity, so if there's anything you want, you should take it now. I've already found something of his that I want to keep. I'll show you."

She went into the bedroom, and I pulled the key out of my purse. When I placed it on the counter Mrs. Markham took a step toward me.

"The apartment manager said Alex was a good tenant. Quiet and polite and always on time with his rent."

She gave me a hungry look, silently begging for tidbits of information about her son. I softened a bit.

"I'm sure he was," I told her. "Alex was one of the nicest people I've ever met. And he had a great sense of humor. He loved to read, and he was a good listener, too." I paused, and then put as much feeling as I could into my voice. "He was my friend. I'm going to miss him more than I can tell you."

She gave me a trembling smile then and a quick nod. "He always did like to read. When he was a little boy, he walked around the house with a book in front of his face. I thought he would trip over the furniture, but he never did."

"Here it is," said Lindsey, returning from the bedroom. "It's Alex's Bible. Look, there are some parts underlined. I'm going to find every one of them and memorize them."

She clutched the Bible to her chest and hugged it. I stood silent for a moment, trying to decide if I should tell her the Bible was mine, not Alex's. The look on her face stopped me. She needed to believe it belonged to her brother. A glance at

Mrs. Markham's face showed me the same. They wanted to believe that Alex had not been alone but had found comfort and solace in the Word of God. Maybe they wanted to believe that Alex had been a Christian and was now in heaven. What harm was there in letting them believe that? I wanted to believe it, too, and I prayed it was true. And like Pastor Paul said, maybe the Lord wouldn't care if we made the assumption that Alex had accepted Jesus at the end.

Anyway, it *was* Alex's Bible. I had given it to him.

I did something out of character then. I stepped toward Lindsey and gave her a hug.

"I think Alex would like that."

Chapter 13

The weeks following Alex's death were hard ones for me. I wish I could say I came to my senses quickly and got on my knees to put things right between God and me, but I didn't. Oh, I prayed, but the void was still there. I shot little arrow prayers across the gap, but I didn't expect God to answer. So, of course, He didn't. Or if He did, I wasn't listening.

I didn't rush right out to get a new Bible, either. I thought about it, most often at night because I had become accustomed to reading it before I fell asleep. The desire to read the Bible wasn't as strong as it had been before, and I didn't want to admit that, so I ignored it.

I'm pretty good at ignoring things I would rather not think about.

Since I wasn't filling my mind with new truth from the Bible, I started slipping back into my old way of thinking. I lost my temper easily. When a supplier at work called to tell me a shipment was going to be a day late, I almost cussed him out. I caught myself right before the words left my mouth, but I felt ashamed that they had even come into my mind. I knew it meant I was losing my grip on my walk with God. Or I would have known if I had allowed myself to think about it.

I dyed my hair again, this time a dark black color called Midnight Satin. It suited my mood. If nothing else, the change would please Mama. Black, at least, was a normal hair color, even if it wasn't mine. When I drove to Salliesburg to check on Mama one Saturday a couple of weeks after Alex's death, she met me at the door with a smile that quickly turned upside-down.

"What have you done to yourself now?" she asked.

My hand came up defensively to touch my ebony head. "You don't like it?"

She pressed her lips tight. "I do not. You look like one o' them Gothers."

"Goths," I corrected, "and I do not."

But her words struck a chord, and I knew I probably did. I wore black slacks, a black tee shirt and a black stud in my nostril. It had been on purpose, of course. I always have been a bit dramatic, even if I can't act.

"Well, my fingernails aren't black, anyway," I said.

"Come on in here and tell me what's wrong."

She backed up to let me by, using her crutch like a pro.

"What makes you think something's wrong?" I asked, irritated. "You're reading too much into appearances, as usual."

She snorted, followed me into the kitchen, and poured herself a cup of coffee. I shook my head when she held the coffee pot toward me and got a can of Diet Coke out of the refrigerator instead. She took a plate out of the cabinet, piled it high with Oreo cookies, and put it on the table between us. Oreos were Mama's version of comfort food.

"I think something's wrong," she told me around a mouthful of cookie, "because you haven't been to church in two weeks—and since you're here on a Saturday morning it means you ain't comin' tomorrow either."

I twisted an Oreo open and licked at the cream filling, as I have done with every Oreo I've ever eaten in my entire life. "I have to work, that's all. Jolene is shorthanded, and I need the money."

"Huh."

We sat silently while each of us went through a couple of cookies. There's something about Mama that just invites me to talk. At least now that I'm an adult there is; as a teenager, I kept plenty of secrets. She sat there, munching and slurping and waiting for me to talk, and before long I chattered like a bird in a cage.

"Actually," I confessed, my gaze fixed on the chocolate cookie pieces in my hand, "I haven't been too enthusiastic about going to church lately."

Mama nodded, as if this was not news to her. "Why is that?"

I shrugged. "I don't know. It just doesn't seem as exciting as it did at first, that's all."

Mama studied the steaming surface of her coffee for a moment.

"Mayla, all of us have times when we have to make ourselves go on. That's true about everything, not just church. After your Daddy died, I had to make myself get outta bed every single morning. You just gotta make yourself keep on goin' no matter what. You gotta set yourself a goal or find a reason that's important to you, and then you head for it no matter what you feel like. Nothin' in this life comes without a struggle. Nothin'. If it was easy, it wouldn't be worth havin'."

I looked up at her. "What was your reason when Daddy died?"

She smiled. "You."

I should have expected Pastor Paul to visit. We had talked several times a week for over a month now, and suddenly my phone calls stopped. Of course he would want to know why. I just didn't expect him to turn up at work.

"You've got a fan," said the hostess a couple of nights after my visit to Mama. "I just seated a guy who asked for your section. Good-looking, too. And no wedding ring. I checked. Table sixty-four."

She winked as she went back to the hostess stand. Curious, I picked up my pen and order pad, looking across the restaurant at sixty-four, and my breath stopped for a moment when I recognized Pastor Paul. He sipped water while studying his menu. I could understand why our hostess would check his ring finger. He was a nice-looking man when he was dressed casually, as he was now. I thought again that there should be a law against preachers wearing jeans. They ought to have to wear something like a priest collar to mark them for what they are.

"Who's the hot guy?" asked Sylvia, coming up behind me from the server's alley. Word spread quickly in that place.

"That's not a hot guy," I told her. "He's my pastor."

She muttered a word under her breath that I couldn't make out, and probably didn't want to know, and went back to the bar. I stood there for a moment, wondering what to say to him. I had skipped church three Sundays in a row, ever since Alex's death.

In fact, the last time we had talked was when I yelled at him in his office. Gathering my courage, I approached his table.

"Well, well, well," I said in a bright voice, "look who's here. No deacon meeting tonight?"

He smiled as if genuinely happy to see me. "I got out of it by sheer luck." He lowered his voice conspiratorially. "Brother Damon said over half of the deacons called with a variety of excuses, but I think it's probably because there's a big boxing match on pay-per-view tonight. I suspect they'll gather someplace where they can yell and cheer without having to put up with the disapproving glare of the preacher."

I chuckled. "If I was a deacon, I'd be dodging the disapproving glare of Brother Damon first. What can I bring you to drink?"

"Diet Coke," he said. "With lemon, if you have it."

"Sure thing. Be right back."

When I returned with his soda, he cocked his head and looked at my hair. "You changed color again."

"Yeah, I do it every so often. Gives Mama something to complain about."

He grinned. "I can imagine. I liked the last one best, I think. That reddish color suited you."

Was that a compliment or an insult? Since it came from Pastor Paul, I decided it was meant kindly, but I ignored it anyway.

"What can I get for you?"

He looked down at his menu. "I've never been here. What's good?"

"The burgers. The Garbage Burger is my favorite."

He gave me a sideways look, skeptical. "Garbage Burger?"

"Yeah, it has a little bit of everything. But it's not for the average guy, you know. You've got to have a spirit of adventure to enjoy The Max's Garbage Burger."

He snapped the menu shut. "I accept your challenge. Bring me a Garbage Burger, all the way. With fries."

"Yes sir!"

He stopped me when I turned to go. "I don't suppose you could take a break and talk to me while it's cooking?"

It was a slow night, and I only had a couple of tables to serve. I could probably get one of the other servers to take them for a few minutes. And besides, I knew he hadn't come all the way to Lexington for a Garbage Burger.

"Let me get your order turned in and I'll take a break."

I punched his order into the terminal in the server's alley, got myself a Coke, and joined him at his table.

"I know why you're here," I told him as I sat in the chair across from him. "I really do plan to come back to church, as soon as they staff up here and I can have Sundays off again."

He cocked his head and studied me for a minute. "I know you will. I've been worried about you, Mayla. The last time we talked, you were pretty upset. How are you holding up?"

"Okay." I played absently with the silverware and avoided his gaze. "I mean, I won't pretend it has been easy, but I'll be okay. It's not like Alex was a lifelong friend or anything. I only knew the guy a few months."

"I wasn't really talking about Alex's death. I was talking about you and your relationship with God. How is that coming along?"

I didn't answer. I couldn't think of a thing to say. The truth was, it wasn't coming along at all. It had stalled, and I didn't want to admit that to him.

"You know, Mayla, we all go through periods when the Christian walk isn't easy. Something like Alex's death can be shattering and can show us things about ourselves that we would rather not face."

I squirmed in my seat. Though Pastor Paul was saying much the same thing Mama had said a few days earlier, he was taking it to a deeper level, and he was closer to the truth than I cared to admit.

"The important thing is that we don't give up. We have to press on toward the goal, like the apostle Paul said. At those times, we need our Christian brothers and sisters around us to encourage us. That's why it's so important to find a place of service. If you've made a commitment to do something in the church, you're less likely to drop away from your relationship with God."

"Well, I don't have a place of service," I said with a touch of bitterness. "It's not because I haven't tried, either."

He leaned back in his chair, grinning. "That's the second reason I wanted to talk to you tonight. I may have a solution to that problem."

A ray of hope flickered inside me. Could this be the goal I needed to get me back on track? "Go on," I told him. "I'm listening."

"I want to do a monthly newsletter, a little magazine that we can mail to everyone on the church's mailing list, telling them what's going on in the church. They used to have one but it got dropped for various reasons before I came three years ago. Only, I want this one to be more than just a newsletter. I want it to have articles and book reviews and devotionals, as well as church events. Even jokes. It should be something people look forward to reading every month, like *Reader's Digest*."

His enthusiasm was contagious. I could picture it, could even see how I would lay it out using the desktop publishing software I had learned in high school. I would need to brush up on my skills, but it wouldn't take long.

He went on. "Sharon just works in the church office a few days a week, and she doesn't have the time to devote to it to really make it good. But you whipped that bulletin out like it was nothing. So I thought maybe you could give it a shot. On a trial basis, just for a few months, to see how you like it and how the church receives it."

"I wouldn't know what to write," I said. "I'm not sure I could come up with enough to fill one page, much less a whole magazine."

"Ah, but you wouldn't have to. I'm sure people in the congregation will submit articles, and you and I will select them together. We could even make assignments to certain people, book reviews for instance. All you would have to do is assemble it, lay it out, and see to the printing and mailing. I'm sure we could get volunteers to handle a lot of the legwork, too."

A grin crept onto my face. "I might be able to handle something like that."

"I've got some budget money stashed away to cover the cost of the first few issues, and by then we'll be into next year's budget cycle. If it goes well, I bet the board will allocate enough money to keep it going." His smile widened. "So is it a deal?"

For the first time in weeks, I felt excited about something. Finally, a service project I could really get into, and maybe even be successful.

I stuck my hand across the table. "It's a deal. When do we start?"

On my lunch hour the next day, I ran over to the Christian bookstore on Nicholasville Road. They had a study Bible just like my old one, and I bought it. After peeling off the cellophane, I fanned the pages and opened it at random. I had never read the book of Hosea, but my eyes were drawn to the first verse of chapter six:

Come, let us return to the L<small>ORD</small>.
He has torn us to pieces
  but he will heal us;
he has injured us
  but he will bind up our wounds.

Tears sprang to my eyes as the words pierced into my soul.

"God, that's just how I feel," I whispered. "I've been torn to pieces. I need you to heal me."

A feeling of peace stole gently over me like a warm breeze on a chilly night. I had a lot of talking to do with God, but at the moment I couldn't say a word. I didn't need to. Instead I sat in my car with my eyes closed and let Him bind up my wounds.

Chapter 14

The more I thought about the church magazine, the more excited I became. Maybe I had finally found my place of service. Maybe God didn't want me to bumble around doing things I wasn't good at and didn't like, such as teaching kids or acting with the drama team.

I had two obstacles, though: money and time. I didn't have a computer, and I couldn't afford to buy one. I planned to buy the desktop publishing software I needed to do the layout work, which was about as far as my budget would stretch. So that meant I would either have to use Mama's computer or the one in the church office. And since I could only install the software on one computer legally, I had to use the same one every time. I decided on Mama's, because

I could kick her off her computer more often than I could impose on Sharon.

As for time, trying to juggle that and two jobs would be a problem. Sunday was the best day because I had decided I needed to start going to church again, but I figured it would take more than one day a week. Mama's computer sat on a desk in a corner of her bedroom, so I couldn't work late at night, as I would have done at home. That left only half a day between church and Mama's bedtime. Saturdays would be great, because then I could have two days in a row, but Fridays and Saturdays were the best days for tips at The Max. Plus, Jolene would probably fire me if I told her I wouldn't work Saturday *or* Sunday.

In the end, I chose Wednesday. I figured I would head to Salliesburg after I got off work and use Mama's computer for a few hours while she attended her Wednesday night Bible study. I could even spend the night there and commute to work in Lexington on Thursday morning.

Jolene rolled her eyes at me when I told her I couldn't work Wednesdays or Sundays, but she let me off without too much hassle. Wednesdays were typically pretty slow.

The following Wednesday, I headed for Salliesburg to install the newly purchased software on Mama's computer. She was expecting me. I got there just as she put supper on the table. She had fixed my favorite meal—pot roast with carrots and onions, mashed potatoes, broccoli casserole, and crescent rolls.

"Mama, you didn't have to cook for me," I told her after we had said the blessing. "You're not planning to do this every Wednesday, are you?"

"'Course not," she said, watching with a satisfied expression as I smothered everything on my plate in thick brown gravy. "But I was in the mood for a big meal tonight, and I couldn't remember the last time I fixed a pot roast."

"Me either." I bit into the tender roast. "Yum. On second thought, you can do this whenever you want."

The washing up didn't take long, and she packaged the left-overs in Tupperware for me to take home the next day. Then she left for church and I went upstairs to get started.

I swear it felt like she came home just ten minutes later. I became so engrossed in designing sample master layouts that I didn't notice three hours slip by. At ten o'clock, Mama walked into the bedroom, startling me so that I nearly jumped out of my skin.

"Lemme see what you've done," she said.

I showed her my samples. I had several styles, but my favorite was a horizontal half-sheet. That way, four pages could be printed on one sheet of paper, folded, and stapled in the center. It looked like a real magazine. I had samples of what the articles would look like, with clip art, sidebars, borders and different font styles to set things off for emphasis. No content, of course, but I copied a sample document from the software tutorial so I would have some text to play around with.

"It's great, baby," she told me, and I could see she meant it. "The church is gonna love this. Tonight, Pastor Paul announced that you're working on it, so I expect people will be sending you articles before too long."

I wasn't finished yet—I could have kept working for hours—but she was ready for bed. I gathered up my samples and kissed her on the cheek.

"Thanks for letting me use your computer, Mama."

"Psht!" She dismissed me with a wave of her hand. "Any time, you know that. Now off to bed with you. I got some e-mails to answer before I go to sleep."

I had a hard time falling asleep that night. My mind kept going over a gazillion ideas for the magazine, and I couldn't relax. So when I got up the next morning, I was groggy. At

6:03 I headed downstairs to grab a cup of coffee, thankful for Mama's automatic coffeemaker. To my surprise, she was already up and sitting at the table, her hair sticking out all around her head and her eyes looking sleepy.

"I've been thinking," she said without preamble as I poured the fragrant coffee into a mug, "that you need your own computer. Much as I like seein' you, it'll be easier to work on your magazine in your own apartment instead of runnin' down here all the time."

"You're right, but I just can't afford it right now. Maybe after I get my car paid off, but—"

"So I'm gonna buy you one."

I was dumbfounded. "You're gonna what?"

"I'm gonna buy you one," she said. "You got a birthday coming up soon, and I've been wonderin' what I was gonna get you. Now I know. I'll get you a computer with a printer and everything. Maybe one of them laptops, so you can bring it here with you if you need to."

I didn't know what to say, so I just stared at her, speechless. I didn't know much about Mama's finances, and I figured she had some of Daddy's life insurance money stashed away for a rainy day, but she sure didn't work at the grocery store for fun. She smiled and stood up, tightening the belt on her cotton bathrobe.

"I looked it up on the Internet last night, and I can get a real good price. I'm gonna order it today and have it shipped to your apartment in Lexington."

I came across the room and grabbed her in a big hug.

"Thank you, Mama. You're awesome, you know that?"

She squeezed me around the neck. "Not really, but I like it when you think so."

I drove to work that morning with a new sense of awe. What an incredible God I had. He gave me a job to do, He saw what I needed to get it done, and He figured out a way to give it to me. And He used the best, most generous mama in the world to do it.

That next Sunday, I returned to church after a month's absence. My little Honda zoomed into the parking lot a few minutes after ten. Throwing the door open, I leaped out of the car and trotted up the sidewalk in something just short of a run. I hate to be late. As I pushed through the glass doors and burst into the entry hall in a rush, I found it occupied by the last person I wanted to see that morning. Mr. Holmes. He stood guard two steps inside the doorway, stopping me dead in my tracks with a glare. Why did I always feel like a little kid caught red-handed at some forbidden act whenever he looked at me from beneath those scraggly gray eyebrows?

"'Morning," I mumbled, forcing myself to look him in the eye as I sidled past at a slower, more dignified pace.

He nodded, and for a moment I thought I would escape scot-free, but just when I had almost made it to the safety of the stairway, he spoke.

"Ain't seen ye in a while."

I turned slowly and looked at him from across the room. "Yeah, I've been kinda busy lately."

His eyelids narrowed as he stared at me, and I wondered if he knew about Alex's death. Surely not. How could he, unless Pastor Paul had told him? I couldn't imagine the preacher would talk about me to the church janitor. Of course, his truck had been in the parking lot that day when I yelled at Pastor Paul in his office. And I had yelled pretty loud.

After a moment, Mr. Holmes gave a curt nod. "Glad yer back."

He turned away then, leaving me to stare at his back with my mouth hanging open. Was I dreaming, or had the grumpiest man in the world just told me he was glad to see me? I shook my head slowly, sure that a minor miracle had taken place right here in the entry hall of Salliesburg Independent Christian Church.

"Thanks," I said to his back before turning toward the stairs and going to join my Sunday school class.

July in Kentucky is nasty. There's just no other way to describe it. Oh, the rain stays away pretty much, which is a welcome change, especially after a wet spring, but the humidity picks up where the rain left off, and that's even worse. I spend the entire month of July going from my air-conditioned apartment to my air-conditioned car to my air-conditioned office. I stay away from the construction sites unless I absolutely can't help it, and if I have to go anywhere I try to do it at night.

Pastor Paul had approved my half-sheet layout and we set the publication date for our first issue of *The Torch* for July 21, my twenty-third birthday. We had argued over the name. I wanted something catchy, like *A Light in the Dark* or *Truth for Our Times*. The preacher favored a more straightforward—and in my opinion, more boring—title, and suggested *The SICC Monthly News*. We settled on *The Torch*, with his favorite as a subtitle in bolded italics.

I called every printer in town and negotiated a bargain rate. We couldn't afford to do color, so I had to work with bolding and shading and different fonts to make it look the way I wanted, but I did manage to talk the man into a glossy cover for the same price as regular paper. We needed to print a hundred and fifty copies so we could have a few extras on hand for giving out to visitors. Pastor Paul snapped a pretty good photograph of the church, which I scanned, and that became the art for the front cover.

The printer's price did not include assembly, so Pastor Paul talked to the youth group and got them to agree to do the assembly as a project at their youth meeting on Sunday the twentieth. He bribed them with the promise of pizza and soda while they worked, but that's okay. Whatever it takes. That meant I had to pick up the printed copies on Saturday. The printer needed at least three days to get the printing done, so we set our drop-dead submission deadline at five o'clock on Tuesday the fifteenth. I would get any last-minute submissions in place that night and take the master to the printer on my way to work Wednesday morning.

The magazine made me something of a celebrity in the church. Our deadline, along with my new e-mail address, was printed in the bulletin every Sunday morning for three weeks, and I developed an electronic relationship with several members of the congregation as they sent me articles, announcements, book reviews and little snippets of news. It was fun to see them at church on Sunday morning after trading e-mails throughout the week.

Very rarely did anyone look twice at my facial jewelry anymore. Even Mrs. Elswick had given up staring pointedly at my lower lip every time we saw each other, especially since she wanted me to include an article about the prayer quilt her Christian sewing circle was working on.

I pored through every magazine I could get my hands on, not to read them but to study the layout and to look for interesting columns and other ideas. I wanted something different, something that would make this new magazine belong to Salliesburg Independent Christian Church exclusively, something that would be of interest to everyone. I thought about a cross-word puzzle or a word search based on Pastor Paul's sermons, but rejected those ideas as being too common. Then, about a week before the deadline, I had a flash of brilliance.

One Wednesday evening, I borrowed Stuart's digital camera and drove to Salliesburg, to a part of town I'd never been in before. I had printed directions from MapQuest on the Internet, and they took me through a neighborhood of small older homes on the west side of town. The late afternoon sun shone through the leaves of untrimmed trees, casting deep shadows across the narrow streets. Finally I pulled into a gravel driveway in front of a single-story white house with a wood plank front porch.

Walking quietly up the three front stairs, I took a deep breath before opening a storm door with a sagging screen to knock on the front door. In a moment I heard the creaking of the floor from inside, and then the door opened a crack and a bloodshot eye peered at me from beneath a bushy gray brow.

"Hello, Mr. Holmes," I said hesitantly. "I came by to see if you would do me a favor. It's about the church magazine."

He opened the door slowly, standing back in the shadows and staring down at me, his face heavy with suspicion. "What kinda favor?"

I took a deep breath. "Well, I've got this idea. I want to have a column called Guess Who? I'll put a baby picture of a church member, along with some interesting facts that nobody would know. That'll be on one of the pages toward the front. Then on the back page, I'll tell everyone who the person is, along with a current picture."

I held up the digital camera for his inspection.

His eyebrows shot upward. "You wanna take a pichur of me?"

"Yes, sir," I told him. "And I'm hoping you have a baby picture you can let me borrow, or at least one of you as a boy. Just to scan. Would you let me do that?"

He seemed to consider my request for a moment, and I could see the merest hint of a smile playing at the corners of his mouth. "Well now, I guiss that'd be okay."

"Great!" We stood for a moment, neither of us moving. "Uh, do you think I could come inside and ask you some questions? Sort of like an interview, you know?"

He shook his head. "Nah, 'at wouldn't be right. We kin jes' talk out here."

He stepped out onto the porch and gestured to one of two green metal chairs on the porch.

I sat in one and gave him a cockeyed look. "Don't tell me you're worried about what the neighbors might say if they see you going inside with a female," I teased.

He snorted, and then actually grinned. "Well, yer a wild 'un, and ye might try somethin' wit me. I gots to protect my honor, ye know."

I laughed out loud, and he joined in. Then I asked about his childhood, and it was like I had opened a floodgate. He talked on and on, telling me about growing up on a farm in northern Tennessee, milking cows and riding on the tractor with his daddy to plow the fields. He told me about Christmas mornings, when he would break the ice in the bucket of water on his dresser, up in his unheated attic bedroom, to wash his face before coming down to the warm kitchen, and finding the table covered with cakes and pies and cookies and candy, every kind of sweet a kid could imagine. I discovered that he'd won the county spelling bee three years running, and that he'd raised and trained bird dogs as a teenager for spending money. I also learned that his wife had grown up on a neighboring farm, and they had gone all the way through school together and had married the day after she graduated from high school.

Before I left, he went inside and got an old shoe box full of yellowed photographs, and we went through them to find one I could use in the magazine. The sun went down and we had to turn the porch light on to see. June bugs buzzed around, occasionally hitting the naked bulb with a little *tap*. I could have sat there listening to his stories all night long.

When I left, he stood on the porch and waved as I drove away.

"Lord," I said as I beeped my horn in farewell, "that was really, really neat. Thank you for Mr. Holmes, and for giving me a new friend where I least expected it."

With a smile on my face, I turned my car onto the main road to return to Lexington.

The magazine's deadline neared, the issue filled, and I had to rearrange the content a dozen times when something new would arrive from someone who insisted on getting their piece in the first issue. I learned a lot, and started making notes of my ideas to make production of the next month's magazine go smoother.

Finally the deadline arrived. I had taken Tuesday night off so I would have plenty of time to work on the final master. I got home and powered up my computer, scanning through the e-mails for the last-minute articles I knew were coming. Everything was there, except—

I picked up the phone and punched in a speed-dial code.

"Hello?"

"Hey, it's me."

"Mayla," said Pastor Paul, "good to hear from you. How's it going? Is everything on schedule?"

"So far so good," I told him. "I'm planning to finish up tonight, but I do have one problem. Someone promised me an article and I haven't gotten it yet. It's now past the deadline, and I'm not sure what to do."

"Well if they can't hit the deadline they may just be too late. We've given everyone plenty of notice. Who is it?"

With a teasing lilt in my voice, I said, "It's you."

He gasped. "I completely forgot! I was supposed to write my pastor letter for inside the front cover."

"That's right."

"I'm so sorry! I can't believe I forgot. I actually have started it, but I put it down last week when I started working on Sunday's sermon and never picked it back up. Would it be okay if I finish it now and e-mail it to you? I'll skip out of the deacon meeting to get it done."

"Really?" I allowed a touch of sarcasm to creep into my voice. "I would hate to make you miss the deacon meeting. I know how you enjoy it."

He snorted. "Yeah, right. Believe me, Brother Damon is more than able to run that meeting, and probably loves the opportunity to do it without me there to interfere. I'll get this done and e-mail it to you. And Mayla?"

"Yeah?"

"I'm so embarrassed. Please forgive me."

I chuckled. "It's okay, really. I should have reminded you last week, but I wanted to see if you would remember on your own."

"I've failed your test then," he said. "I promise to do better next time."

"I'm sure you will. E-mail it to me as soon as you finish. G'night."

"Good night, Mayla."

✝

I was so excited when I left the printer that Saturday morning. The cover looked great, just like a real magazine. The magazine consisted of four two-sided sheets, for a total of sixteen magazine pages. The printer had put them in a box with colored paper separating each page, ready to be collated and assembled by the youth group the following evening. I had already gotten the mailing list from Sharon and had printed address labels on my printer, so they were ready to be stuck to the finished magazines and mailed.

I called Pastor Paul to tell him how good they looked.

"I'm afraid we have a problem," he told me.

"What kind of problem?"

"A couple of weeks ago, the youth group was invited to attend an interfaith skating party tomorrow night, so they won't be available to do the assembly."

My temper flared. "But they promised!"

"I know, but Nikki didn't make a note on their activity calendar and when the invitation came they forgot. It's not a disaster, though. Brother Damon and I already talked about it, and the deacons will do it on Tuesday night. How long can it take with ten people working together? We'd be glad to help out."

"Then it won't go out until Wednesday, three days late. Our very first issue will miss the publication date we announced."

The preacher's voice was infuriatingly calm. "Three days isn't a disaster. Besides, the date was only a target, not a hard deadline. If we're a few days late it's not a big deal."

I sat there in the car with my fists clenched, trying to calm myself down. He was right. It wasn't a big deal, but I was still irritated. I had worked so hard to make sure everything was perfect, and I really wanted it mailed on my birthday.

"I work Tuesday night," I told him, pleased that my voice sounded nearly as calm as his. "I can't be there to show you how it's supposed to be done."

"You can put together a sample and we'll figure it out. Mayla, don't worry. You've done your part. Now turn it over to me and let me handle it from here."

There didn't seem to be anything else to say, so we hung up. Sulking, I put the car in gear and backed out of my parking place.

"Lord, I just don't know why people can't do what they say they're going to do," I complained aloud as I drove. "It makes me mad. If I told someone I would help with a project, I would do it. Now I'm going to miss my deadline. It's just not fair!"

Then I had an idea. Pastor Paul said the project wouldn't take long with ten people working together, and he was right. Still, there were only a hundred fifty copies of five pages that needed to be collated, folded, stapled, sealed, and labeled. I could probably knock that out in a few hours when I got off work at nine. If I got it done, I could take them to church in the morning and put them in the Fellowship Hall for people to pick up their own copy to save the church the cost of postage. I could not only make my mailing deadline, I could be a day early.

I put my turn signal on and whipped the car around, heading for Wal-Mart on Richmond Road. I needed supplies!

"What's all this?" asked Sylvia, her dark hair sticking up all over the place as she walked out of her bedroom yawning and tying the belt on her bathrobe.

I had commandeered the dinette table and had my night's work ready to go. The path around the table had been cleared, the chairs pushed back against the walls so I would be free to walk around my assembly line. Five piles of paper were laid out in order, then an empty space where I would fold them, then the stapler I had just bought at Wal-mart loaded with staples and ready to go, then a tape dispenser for sealing the assembled magazine, and finally the alphabetized mailing labels. On one chair nearby was the first of the boxes for the magazines to be stored, their alphabetical order intact, for transport to the church in the morning.

"Don't touch anything," I warned as she eyed the pieces of my carefully laid out project. "The youth group ducked out on me so I've got to put the thing together myself. I'm going to do it when I get off work tonight, so this will be clean by morning, I promise."

She walked around the table, picking up a page and glancing through it.

"Looks pretty good," she commented. "But this is going to take you all night."

Feeling a thrill of satisfaction at her compliment, I shrugged. "Nah, just most of it. It's okay. I'll take a nap tomorrow afternoon."

She replaced the sheet of paper, tidied the stack, and walked wordlessly into the kitchen for coffee. I gave the table one final satisfied look before I left for the restaurant.

When I got off at nine, I hurried home, eager to get started. The first few went slowly; the stapler was going to be a problem. The arm wasn't long enough to fit to the middle of the crease so the folded pages had to be scrunched up a bit to get the staples in the center. Feeling stupid for not checking the length before I bought it, I spent a few precious minutes trying to figure out the best way to get the task done while keeping the collated pages neat.

Someone knocked on the door.

"C'mon in," I shouted, putting the fifth completed magazine carefully into the box.

The door opened and in walked Michael, Tattoo Lou, and Heidi. Stuart followed, carrying three pizza boxes. The aroma of hot pepperoni and sausage filled the apartment almost immediately.

"Surprise!" he shouted, setting the pizza on the sofa table and crossing the room with outstretched arms to hug me. "We came to help you celebrate your birthday."

"Guys, I really appreciate it but I don't have time for a party right now," I told them. "I've got this thing I'm trying to get done."

"We know," said Heidi. "Sylvia told Stuart about it this afternoon and said you would probably appreciate some help. It's our birthday present to you."

Lou held up a couple of two-liters, one Diet Coke and the other Dr. Pepper.

"We even brought soda to drink instead of beer, since this is a church project and all, but I'm switching to beer as soon as it's done."

He set the drinks beside the pizza.

Gratitude washed over me. "You guys are the best."

"Yeah, we know," grinned Michael. "Now, what do you want us to do?"

I gave them each a task. Michael assembled the pages and handed the collated stack to Stuart, who folded them in the center. Then I stapled each one twice and handed it to Lou for sealing. Heidi slapped a label in the appropriate place and filed it in the box. Within a few minutes, there was a growing pile in front of me, because the stapling process was such a slow one.

Lou watched me for a minute, then stepped in and took my stapler.

"I have an idea," he said. "I'll be back in a few minutes. You guys keep working."

We all switched to assembling for the fifteen minutes Lou was gone, and by the time he returned we had a lot of collating done. He came through the door with the oddest-looking contraption I've ever seen. He had gotten a second stapler from somewhere, more beat up than my new one, opened them both flat and screwed them to a board about a foot square. He had removed the little plates from the base of the staplers and fixed them in place beneath the staple head so the staples would seal.

"I think I got the spacing about right," he said, picking up one of our collated and folded magazines and sliding it onto the board.

It was perfect. We marked guidelines with a pencil on the wood, and Lou took over the stapling task, going through our backlog in almost no time.

We had a lot of fun. We turned on the stereo, and Stuart kept us entertained by dancing around the assembly line. Occasionally, someone would take a break to eat a slice of pizza, and the rest of us would switch jobs, which kept everyone from getting bored. In just under two hours we had finished all one hundred fifty magazines, plus a few extras.

"You guys are great," I told them, sitting on the couch afterward.

Heidi sat cross-legged on the floor in front of the coffee table, munching on lukewarm pizza. Stuart and Michael lounged on the couch beside me, and Lou sat in the recliner, sipping his beer and thumbing through one of the extra magazines. Now that was a sight I never thought I would see—Lou, with his tattoo-covered arms sticking out of a ripped No Fear tee shirt with a red-eyed fiend plastered across his chest, reading a Christian magazine. I wondered what Mama's Tuesday night ladies' group would think about that.

"Hey, it says here you guys have a softball team," he commented. "I used to play softball in high school."

"I'm sure they could use you. The guy who runs it told me they're the worst team in the league."

He gave me a cynical look over the top of the magazine. "Can you see me at a church softball game? I'll bet they don't even have beer at the concession stand."

Everyone laughed, and then Stuart stood up. The others got to their feet as well.

"A bunch of guys are going over to Rob's tonight. You want to come?" asked Michael.

I glanced at the clock. A quarter till twelve. "Nah," I told him, "I've got to get up early. But listen, you guys, thanks. That would have taken me all night without you."

They each hugged me and told me happy birthday.

"Hey," said Heidi as she walked through the door into the cool night air, "we just did a good deed for a church. Do you think we get brownie points in heaven for that?"

The guys laughed, but I nodded. "I wouldn't be surprised. Someone told me once that no act of kindness goes unrewarded."

Sylvia came in at one-thirty after closing the restaurant. I was waiting for her, curled up on the couch proudly reading through my finished product for the third time. I had cleaned the apartment and had even taken the empty pizza boxes out to the Dumpster.

"Hey," I said as she locked the door behind her.

She looked around. "You finished?"

"Thanks to my helpers. And thanks to you for recruiting them."

She shrugged. "I've seen how hard you worked on this, and I figured you could use some help. I would have done it but I had to work."

I raised my eyebrows. "You? Help with a *church* project?"

She gave me a stern look. "I would have been helping with a *friend's* project."

She dropped sideways into the recliner with her legs hanging over the arm, her size five shoes swinging two feet above the floor.

"Well I appreciate it," I said, "and especially coming from you. I'm glad we're still friends."

She leaned back, staring up at the ceiling, dark hair hanging over the other arm of the chair. She spoke without looking at me.

"I used to go to church, you know."

"I figured you did, since you can quote the Bible better than me."

"I was the Bible Bingo champion two years in a row at church camp. Camp Calvary." She was quiet for a few breaths. "I loved church camp."

This conversation was completely unexpected, and I had to tiptoe into it, feeling my way in the dark. Given our relationship over the past two months I knew everything could turn unexpectedly with one wrong word. *Lord,* I prayed, *don't let me say the wrong thing.*

"I've never been," I told her. "What do you do at church camp?"

"Oh, you play games, team games mostly, like volleyball, softball, relays, even Ping-Pong and shuffleboard. At Camp Calvary, we had teams and whenever you won something you got points. The last night, they gave awards—medals and ribbons, stuff like that. Every day, you had classes outside in the woods where we sat on log benches under the trees. Every night, we had a big bonfire and sang songs, then went to sleep on bunk beds in a big dormitory room, all the girls in one building and the boys in another. I always had a top bunk. A bunch of kids from my church went, but so did kids from churches all over the state. It was fun to see old friends every summer. I was really into church back then."

She fell silent, staring at the ceiling and swinging her feet.

"So what happened?" I asked. "Why did you stop going?"

"I found out that most people who call themselves Christians aren't."

I didn't know what to say, so I said nothing. She was quiet a long time.

"My father was an elder in our church," she said, her voice soft. "He served communion, took up the offering, sang in the choir. He even filled in for the minister once when he was out of town. He was a real 'godly man,' everyone thought. Then he would come home, and at night he would come into my bedroom. For as long as I can remember, I got midnight visits from him, even as a really little girl. I thought it was normal, you know, that every father did those things with his daughter. Till I got old enough to learn a name for it, and I found out that child abuse is illegal."

The room grew very quiet. I prayed as hard as I could, begging God to give me wisdom like He'd given Solomon, something to say that would be just exactly the right thing. But I felt as if my mouth were glued shut.

"So when I was thirteen I went to my minister. I told him what was going on. He was horrified, of course. He prayed with me, told me he would take care of it. He must have done something, because the nighttime visits stopped. But nothing else happened. Nothing. No one ever mentioned it again. My father still sang in the choir, still served communion, still collected the offering. And he never spoke another word to me as long as he lived."

"And your mom?" I asked in a quiet voice.

Sylvia shrugged. "We've never discussed it. I don't know if the minister told her or not. At the time I thought he probably hadn't, because surely she would have talked to me about it. Now when I think about it, I figure she must have known. How could she not? She lived right there in the same house, and it went on for years. I guess she couldn't handle knowing, so she ignored it."

We sat silent for a long time. I stole a glance at Sylvia and saw a few tears slide down her face and disappear into her hair, but she kept her gaze fixed on the ceiling. I wanted to come up with an explanation, something that would defend Christians but not sound like I was excusing the horrible crime done to her. At the moment, I was too horrified to think of anything except that I would like to find that minister and put a couple of bullet holes in him for the damage he had done. Her father, being dead, was beyond my reach, or I would have come up with a number of appropriate punishments for him, too.

When I finally did speak, I was careful to keep my voice steady. "Thank you for telling me. That explains a lot. No wonder you flipped out when I got baptized. I don't think I'd want to live with a religious nut either, if I were you."

"I wouldn't have told you at all, but you surprised me. I've watched, and you're not putting on a show. If it had been just an outside change, you would have taken out the labret and nostril studs, dyed your hair back to your natural color, and started trying to look different. But for you it wasn't about that. It's real to you."

"Yes, it is."

She turned suddenly and caught me in a direct gaze.

"So what's the difference? How is your church different from the one I grew up in?"

Lord, this is it. Don't let me screw this up.

"I doubt if my church is different. Except," I hurried on, "I think my pastor is different from that minister. But I'm sure there are people in my church who do bad things, even terrible things, and if I caught them I'd be the first to string them up by their toes and beat the tar out of them."

She gave a sour grin at my vehemence.

"But," I continued, "that doesn't have anything to do with what has happened to me. I didn't just join a church two months ago. I met Jesus. What I have isn't a membership card, it's a relationship with a real Man, the Savior. That's truer and deeper than any church or preacher, and it's the realest thing I've ever found."

A month before, Sylvia would have fired a sarcastic comment back at me. Heck, a month before I wouldn't have been able to say those words to her, wouldn't have known how to articulate what I felt. Now they were exactly the right words at exactly the right time, and God Himself used them to touch her aching heart.

Sylvia slowly twisted around in the chair until she sat straight, her feet flat on the floor, looking directly into my eyes.

"I want that, Mayla. I want to meet that Man."

And right there, at two o'clock in the morning, in our living room, Sylvia met her true Father, the one who loves her more than any of us can ever know. She prayed the prayer that changes lives, and we both wept as God healed her wounds and gave her a brand-new life.

Chapter 15

I don't think I have ever had a prouder moment than I did that Sunday morning when Sylvia and I marched through the doors of the church carrying one hundred fifty copies of *The Torch*. Pastor Paul caught sight of us and came over immediately.

"Mayla! You've already done it!"

He picked up one of the magazines and examined the cover with admiration.

"It looks wonderful. Awesome. Did you do all of them yourself?"

"No, I had the help of some really good friends," I told him, grinning over my shoulder at Sylvia. "And here's one of them. Sylvia Thomas, this is Pastor Paul Rawlings."

"Sylvia, I'm so happy to meet you." Pastor Paul took the box from her, set it on the announcement table and held out his hand. "And also to welcome you to Salliesburg Independent Christian Church. We're glad you've come to visit with us this morning."

"Well actually, Sylvia isn't here just to visit," I told him, grinning so wide my jaws hurt. "She became a Christian last night, and she's here to get baptized."

Pastor Paul's face split wide, and he gave a joyous laugh. Then he rushed forward and grabbed one of Sylvia's hands in both of his. I saw her wince as he squeezed, and I smothered a grin as I remembered his overly exuberant welcome-to-the-kingdom grip.

"Praise God!" he nearly shouted, drawing stares from everyone. "Praise God forevermore!"

Sylvia laughed, whether from embarrassment or from pure joy I couldn't tell. Probably some of both.

It was one of the happiest moments of my life when I stood in that robe room in exactly the same place my mama had stood just two months before, watching as Pastor Paul baptized my best friend. When Sylvia came up out of that water, I swear her face shined like Moses' when he came down off the mountain. I was even more excited for her than I had been for myself, and that's saying something. It was hard not to give a cheer. I settled instead on wrapping her in a big, fluffy towel and hugging the breath right out of her.

While she changed into dry clothes—it helps to know when you're going to be baptized and you can come prepared—I went out into the sanctuary and was immediately swamped with people congratulating me on *The Torch*. Everyone said it was the best magazine they had ever read. Mrs. Elswick said it was even better than *Reader's Digest*. Mr. Holmes came over with a big grin on his face and told me a kid had asked for his autograph.

I thought about how much Alex would have enjoyed hearing about this day. Then I found myself smiling. Maybe he was enjoying it from heaven.

The next day was my birthday. I got to work and laughed when I saw how Alison had decorated my desk. She must have come in over the weekend and spent a couple of hours doing it. Streamers hung like a waterfall from the ceiling above my desk so that I couldn't move without pink crepe paper brushing my face. Confetti covered the entire surface of my desk and chair, and about a million little smiley faces had been pinned up on the divider that separated me from the front door. A big banner wishing me "Happy Birthday *Mayla!*" had been strung across the front, my name printed neatly in bold black letters.

Alison came in a few minutes later, carrying a cake and singing "Happy Birthday" at the top of her voice.

She deposited the cake on the center of my desk, fished a brightly wrapped box out of her purse, and handed it to me with a wide grin.

"Go ahead, open it now," she insisted.

I did. Inside was a candle holder shaped like a scroll with a white votive candle in the base beside it. The scroll bore the words, "Let your light shine before men. Matthew 5:16."

"Hey, this is great," I told her. "I like it a lot."

"I hoped you would," she said, grinning ear to ear. "I got it because I think you do that—let your light shine, I mean. You did for me, anyway."

Just two months before, Alison wouldn't have given me the time of day, and now she was showering me with gifts. God does amazing things when we let Him have His way.

"Thank you, Alison," I said, genuinely touched.

It was a great day. Mr. Clark and Mr. Hasna sent me a big bouquet of flowers, and Mama sent a bundle of helium balloons delivered by a clown with the worst singing voice I've ever heard. He had the whole office in stitches with his jokes. Everyone who came into the office got a piece of cake and wished me happy birthday, and I felt like a princess. It was a new feeling for me.

The best gift of all came at home in the mail. It was a card, with a return address in Orlando. My grandmother's address. I ripped open the envelope, pleased that Aunt Louise had remembered my birthday. When I opened it and saw the signature, my breath stopped.

Happy birthday, Granddaughter, it read. *I'd be glad if you came for a visit sometime. It's long overdue. Love, Grandmother.*

I cried like a baby.

Twenty-three years old. I could remember being thirteen, standing in front of the bathroom mirror and wondering what I would look like in ten years. Would the pimples finally be gone? (They were.) Would I finally have a woman's breasts? (I didn't.) Would my hair be the same dull brown? (Obviously not.) I studied my reflection now, knowing that my younger self could not possibly have guessed the changes I would undergo years later. Oh, the hair and the piercings were only part of the story. I was changed, really changed, and the changes that had taken place inside of me had overflowed into the world around me.

I examined my hair critically. The black didn't really suit me. Pastor Paul had said he preferred Black Cherry, but somehow I wasn't in the mood for that again. In fact, I realized with something of a shock that I was in the mood these days to look . . . well, less extreme. I opened the cabinet door, pulled out a dark brown towel and wrapped it around my head. Turning this way and that, I decided it wouldn't look too bad. Maybe it was time.

But if my hair was a normal color, the labret stud would look out of place. I stared at it a long time, remembering the way I had felt when I'd first had it done. Bold. Free. Independent. A bit naughty. Radical. It had symbolized all those things, and I had enjoyed that image for a whole year, every minute of it.

Now, I didn't want to be a radical anymore. I was different, and that difference needed a chance to be seen without people getting distracted before they noticed. I removed the stud from beneath my lower lip and placed it on the counter. There was a hole and I would probably always have a scar, but it was a little one. Not really noticeable if you weren't looking for it.

I adjusted the towel and examined my reflection once more. Yes, that was the look for me. But I would never be satisfied being completely normal. The nostril stud would stay.

On Sunday, Sylvia drove to Salliesburg with me. It had been exciting to see the changes in her over the past week. Not physical changes, but real, deep spiritual changes. She smiled more than I had ever seen in all the time I've known her. She radiated peace, like she was a bonfire and peace was the heat flowing out of her.

She wasn't shy, either. I got up one morning to go to work, shocked to find her sitting in the living room with Tattoo Lou, her Bible opened in her lap, preaching up a storm. She had hooked up with him after work, brought him home to tell him her story, and kept him up all night. He hadn't asked Jesus into his heart yet, but she was so determined I figured it was only a matter of time.

That Sunday was a hot July day, the sun working over-time even at nine-thirty in the morning. The humidity was already around ninety percent, and sweat plastered my blouse to my back on the walk from the car to the church. Sylvia and I walked through the door, thankful for the blast of air-conditioning that hit us in the face.

Mama took one look at me and threw her hands up in the air.

"Praise the Lord for brown hair!" she shouted, drawing stares from the dozen or so people standing nearby.

Then she looked closer and noticed the missing labret stud, and a wide grin split her face in two. I held up my hand before she could shout again.

"Please, Mama," I whispered, self-conscious from the curi-ous looks and smiles I was getting. "Don't make a scene."

Mama grabbed me and hugged me to her chest, nearly squeezing the breath right out of me in the process.

"I'm just so happy," she said. "Now we can move forward with our plan."

Alarm gripped me. If Mama had a plan that required me to remove my labret stud, maybe I had acted too hastily.

"What plan?" I asked warily.

She pulled my arm through hers and locked her other arm through Sylvia's. We were dragged toward the sanctuary like dogs on a leash as she spoke in a conspiratorial whisper.

"Well, Sara Marie Tucker, she's in my Tuesday night ladies' group you know, has a son who's twenty-seven and he don't have a girlfriend so we've been tryin' to—what?"

I had stopped short and jerked my arm away from hers.

"Don't go there," I warned.

She gave me one of those innocent looks that was any-thing but.

"Now that you don't look like you just dropped your Uzi after the last bank job, you'd be perfect for him!"

Sylvia was trying hard not to laugh, but I didn't see anything funny about being one of Mama's little projects. I had been there before.

"Listen," I whispered urgently, "I can find my own dates, thank you very much. I don't want to go out with Sara Marie Tucker's son, so you can just tell the Tuesday night ladies they can find another victim."

I must have convinced her, because she turned her eager eye on Sylvia. "What about you, honey? You got a boyfriend?"

Sylvia quickly dropped her arm and took a step backward. "Thanks, but I'm not interested."

"Huh." Mama sniffed, momentarily stalled, but if I knew her, not defeated. "Well anyway, you look beautiful, baby. 'Fore you know it you're gonna be beatin' the men off with a stick."

Later, sitting in the second row, between Sylvia and Mama, I did some serious thinking, and not about Pastor Paul's sermon, either. Mama's plan kept rolling around in my mind. The fact was, I used to date a lot, but since becoming a born-again child of God, I really wasn't interested in dating. Life was too new and exciting, and there was too much to learn. What I needed now wasn't romance; I needed friends who would help me learn.

I glanced sideways at Sylvia. She caught my gaze briefly and smiled, then returned her attention to the pulpit. I looked the other way where Mama sat with her brow creased, listening to the sermon and nodding in agreement. Turning slightly in my seat, I saw Mr. Holmes standing in his usual place in the back corner of the sanctuary. I thought of Alison. The Lord had fixed me up in the friends department pretty well.

Raising my head, I looked toward the front of the church. Pastor Paul had walked out from behind the pulpit, his hands gesturing to emphasize a point. Even from where I sat in the congregation, I could see the excitement in his eyes as he preached the Word of God to God's people.

Someday, Lord, I found myself saying silently, *I'm going to feel like dating again. And when I do . . . if he's still available. . . .*

Blushing to the hair roots, I did as the apostle Paul suggested and took that thought captive. But I didn't banish it completely. I just tied it up and threw it in the back of my mind until the time came to bring it out again.

Someone pounded on the door at ten o'clock that night. Sylvia and I had just returned home from a Sunday night Bible study in Salliesburg after spending the afternoon at Mama's house.

"Grab that, will you?" Sylvia said as she went into the bedroom to change clothes.

It was Stuart.

"I've been watching for you to come home," he said, pushing through the doorway uninvited. "I have a favor to ask."

I eyed him suspiciously. "What kind of favor?"

"A big one," he admitted, tilting his head and fixing me with a wide-eyed look of innocence. "I promise, it's right up your alley."

"Up my alley, huh? Okay, what do you need?"

"It's not me. It's this guy I know, and he's gotten in a lot of trouble. I think he needs a friend. His family has pretty much abandoned him."

This sounded familiar. "Another guy who needs a friend, huh? Does this one have AIDS?"

Stuart looked shocked. "Bradley? No! He's not even gay. He's in prison."

"Prison!" I took an involuntary step backward. "You've gotta be kidding!"

Stuart folded his hands beneath his chin to plead. "Please, Mayla? He doesn't have anyone else, and he's really lonely. Just one visit is all I ask. Aren't Christians supposed to visit people in prison?"

I couldn't help it. I rolled my eyes. "You remember that from Sunday school, do you?"

"I have a very good memory," he assured me. "So you'll do it?"

I didn't answer immediately. *Lord, is this something You want me to do?* I asked silently. *'Cause I don't know how good I'll be at it.* Then I thought of Alex, and how uneasy I'd felt before my first visit to the hospital.

"You know," I told Stuart, "you keep finding me these little 'projects' to handle, but one day I just might turn you into the next one."

He gave me a startled look, then grinned. "Does that mean you'll do it?"

I sighed. "Yeah, I'll do it."

He clapped his hands and pulled a folded piece of paper from his jeans. Thrusting it toward me he said, "Here's his name and directions for getting in to see him. Thanks, Mayla, you're a doll."

I shut the door behind him and leaned against it, shaking my head.

Okay, God, I'm going to prison. I hope You know what You're getting me into.

Deep inside I could almost feel the Lord chuckling, and I couldn't help smiling along with Him. I was getting ready to take another big step down the path He had laid out for me, and I suddenly realized I couldn't wait to get started.